EASY TARGETS

"FIRE!" Eli Holten shouted above the tumult of galloping horses and Apaches discharging rifles.

Three warriors were swept from their mounts. Two horses died. Red Head and Alchise looked on in disbelief as the whites rallied and continued to direct accurate fire into the ranks of the attackers. Stung by the insult of defeat, yet unwilling to risk more men, Red Head called off his band and they rode swiftly out of sight.

"That's it for now," the scout remarked. "We managed to hold off two charges. We've plenty of ammunition in the wagon."

"Problem is, how do we take it with us?" Carlos O'Banyon queried. "Two of the mules are dead and half the horses. We're as good as on foot."

Checking quickly, Eli verified this gloomy report. They could use surviving horses to pull the wagon, the mules would do for pack animals, yet that literally left all but himself and Ed Hendrickson afoot. They would, the scout grimly acknowledged, be easy targets if the Apaches decided to attack again. And there was no doubt in the scout's mind that they would . . .

#28

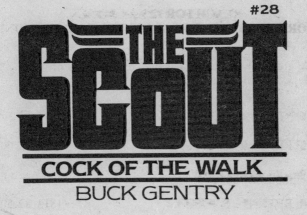

THE SCOUT

COCK OF THE WALK

BUCK GENTRY

ZEBRA BOOKS
KENSINGTON PUBLISHING CORP.

We gratefully acknowledge the contributions of
Mark K. Roberts to this work.

ZEBRA BOOKS

are published by

Kensington Publishing Corp.
475 Park Avenue South
New York, NY 10016

First printing: December, 1988

Printed in the United States of America

This volume in the adventures of Eli Holten is dedicated with respect and camaraderie to Bill Johnstone. Your Mountain Man *is superb.*
—BG

"The first explorers of the West were, of course, Indians. The Sioux, then the Delawares and Cherokees. They had been forced out by the expansion of Anglo civilization. Often called 'breeds' or 'half-breeds' by whites, the Delawares and Cherokees in particular became the first frontier scouts."

—Robert J. Conley
"Early Explorers of the West"
WWA Convention, 1988

CHAPTER 1

With short bursts of energy the small, dusty-tan lizard swiftly darted from the shade of the giant sagauro cactus to the pool of darkness under an overhanging rock, then to the twilight dimness created by a stunted paloverde. It paused, throat palpitating as the little creature sucked in the hot, dry Arizona air. Behind the panting saurian, cactus wrens quarreled over a thick grub their industrious excavating had uncovered in the pipe organ cactus. The spiny-backed reptile tensed for another rush. Dust spurted from under clawed feet.

A black, forked tongue flickered once to test the air, then the horrible needle-toothed jaws closed with an audible *snap!* Hind legs and tail protruding from one side of the gila monster's fatal grin, the lizard swung its head from side to side. The beaded jaw of the monster moved forward and back with the regularity of a shuttle cock, forcing wounds to open and the creature's lethal venom into the prey's system. Bright yellow eyes dimmed, vitality escaping, and the tiny lizard stilled. The monstor shook its head, positioning the meal in line with its gullet, a sudden gulp and even the tail disappeared into the lipless mouth. A moment later, the gila monster's head developed a hole where its left ear should have been. The opposite side of the skull bulged outward a fraction of time before the thin bone gave way and showered the thirsty land with blood and fluids.

"Not a hell of a lot else to do," Eli Holten remarked casually to his companion as he lowered his smoking Remington revolver.

Eagerness lighted Lt. Tommy Cruse's face. "We could go into Globe and, ah, visit the ladies, Eli," he prompted.

Eli pulled a sour face. "Right now I'm about ladied out."

"*Señorita* Esmeralda?" Cruse questioned, naming the scout's latest light of love. "I don't know how anyone could get tired of her."

Frown wrinkles gullied Holten's brow. "You don't have to listen to her constantly harping about marriage."

"What's so bad about marriage?" Lieutenant Cruse inquired, his youthful idealism slightly stung.

"Tommy, my young friend, man is not by nature monogamous. He is a hunter, a rover, an experimenter, and . . ."

Expecting this profound observation to lead to an extraordinary philosophical revelation, Tommy Cruse leaned forward, absorbing, sponge-like, Eli Holten's every word.

"A stiff prick has no conscience," the scout concluded.

"Ummh!" Tommy exploded. "I swear, Eli, I never know when you're serious or not. We'd better be heading back to the post."

"What for? To watch ol' Charlie Gatewood put his Apache scouts through their paces? As for being serious, I was old son, I certainly was."

10

Tommy raised an eyebrow in doubting response. "You've said yourself that the Apaches make fine scouts. What's wrong with Captain Gatewood drilling his men?"

"If left to their natural instincts, the Apaches make excellent scouts," Holten answered. "They don't do well at close order drill and parade ground didoes. They'd rather shoot at moving things than paper targets. That's why you rarely see the Kid and my other six Apaches around the Post. They're out doing what they do best."

His expression changed to wonder, Lieutenant Cruse spoke with appreciation. "It seems I've had a lecture in scouting techniques. All the same, we ought to get back. If you're going to keep an eye on what's going on, you can't do it from here."

Holten produced a blank expression. "What are you talking about?"

"General Crook left his two best scouts behind when he went on campaign. Al Sieber is at Camp McDowell and you're here at Camp Thomas. If the General thought all was well in the garrisons and that the reservation would carry on at San Carlos with business as usual, he wouldn't have done that."

"You're a perceptive little devil, Tommy," Holten complimented the youthful officer's deductive ability. "With how many of the others have you discussed this theory of yours?"

Cruse looked disappointed. "I've kept it to myself, Eli."

"Good. I, ah, suggest you continue to do so. You're right about one thing, though. We might as well go back to the menagerie."

A twenty minute ride brought the pair to the waist-high earthen wall that surrounded a collection of stained and weather-aged tents which comprised Camp Thomas. On the rough-hewn parade ground, a formation of sullen, hot, dirty, and sweaty Apache scouts, in regulation blue trousers and shell jackets went through the paces of dismounted drill. They made not even halfhearted attempts at keeping in step. Their shoulders swayed and heads bobbed. A short distance away a white man, in the uniform of a captain, glared at them, fists on hips.

"Send them on a deer hunt, Charlie," the scout suggested as he reined in beside Capt. Charles Gatewood. "Or have them round up a hundred rabbits for the mess hall. You'll get a lot better cooperation out of them that way."

Gatewood's lips curled in disgust. "What do you know about it, Holten? You're new to this part of the country. You've never been to West Point and you've no qualifications to command troops. You might spoil your own scouts, but mine, by God, are going to learn to soldier."

Not alone in his dislike of the highly recommended northern plains Indian fighter, Gatewood felt encouraged in expressing his scorn to the fullest. Charles Gatewood and several of Crook's officers saw Eli Holten as an interloper. Even a couple of seasoned scouts, senior in time on the desert, had considered the vacancy as Al Sieber's number two as their sinecure. Holten's arrival dispelled this ambition. They likewise joined the Eli Holten hate club. Holten dismissed this wisdom as he looked about the makeshift outpost.

"Trash wasn't buried, there's still a break in the south wall. Was water carted up from the stream?" he listed the readily visible sins of omission.

Gatewood bristled. "You're a civilian contract scout, Holten, not an officer of the United States Army. You'll give no orders around here. How we run this post is strictly between us and General Crook."

Holten produced a smile that bordered on sweetness. "Yes. It most certainly is. Now, if my services are no longer needed for the forseeable future, I think I'll take a few days in Globe."

Gatewood furrowed his brow. "You can go to Globe or straight to hell for all I care."

"Why thank you, Charlie. I'll take that as leave to depart from the post."

Wooden slats and rawhide strings served as springs for the bed. They creaked in descant rhythm to the erotic sounds that came from the lunging couple on the cotton-stuffed mattress.

"Aaah! Ooooh! Ummmm! Ah-ah-ah!" crooned the lovely Esmeralda Escobar.

There was no doubt about it — nothing felt better than to be in Eli's powerful embrace, letting him explore her velvety flesh arousing her to the heights of sensuous delights. With all his might he drove into her, hips pistoning as he carried them toward riotous completion. Esmeralda began to toss her head from side to side and gasp for breath. With both hands she grasped his bare buttocks and pulled him closer.

"Oh, oh!" she cried in ecstatic release.

"Some time," he panted. "Some time you'll make me so dizzy I'll not come out of it."

"Then you'll have to marry me so I can take care of you," Esmeralda murmured.

Eli winced. Then, in a sweet trance of lethargy they disengaged. Esmeralda gazed along the scarred, lean, muscular expanse of the blond haired scout. Her hand slowly followed.

"You're so lovely, she purred. "I want you with me . . . always. Say yes, Eli. Please say yes."

"Yes," the bemused Eli answered.

Instantly Esmeralda brightened and began to manipulate him with more earnest strokes. "Oh, darling, then you *will* marry me."

"No!" Eli shouted. "I didn't mean . . . I thought you wanted to . . ."

Esmeralda pouted.

Responding despite his mood, Eli's penis swelled to new life, firm and ready for yet another encounter. Their fourth since he arrived in Globe late that evening. Esmeralda bent low over him and her tongue inscribed exciting spirals across his hardened flesh.

"See what you'd be missing if we don't get married?"

Instantly Eli went limp. Something, he decided in amorous agony, had to be done about this. Perhaps if he were to take her back to her family in Sonora?

While a frantic Esmeralda tried to raise the dead, Eli savored the idea. Yes, that might indeed do it. They could share their pleasure along the way and then he could deliver her into the hands of Don Francisco Escobar at the family hacienda and ride off into the sunset. The more he thought of it, the more Eli liked the idea.

Disgruntled the Apache scouts at Camp Thomas might be. Angry best described Dos-Tan-Nanta, the

Apache war leader with the slight coppery cast to his hair. He had for too long chaffed at the inactivity, inadequate and often spoiled rations, mistreatment, and malarial swamp along the Gila River at this place called San Carlos. He would endure no more, the man the whites called Red Head decided. Walking swiftly among the wikiups, tents and ramshackle cabins of the agency he summoned certain men with a look, or a nod. When they all gathered at a tall flat rock atop a high, red mesa, Dos-Tan-Nanta spoke his mind.

"My brothers we have tried the whiteman's way. It is a path that leads only to early death. Our children starve, or are taken from us in the fever that abounds in this place. We're given rotten food and little of it. Juh, Geronimo, and others have already left this accursed place. The soldier-chief Crook seeks them now. It's our turn to make the *pen-dik-olye* pay for the treatment they've given us."

Agreement went among those gathered. One in particular, Alchise, nodded his head vigorously and took a step forward, a signal that he wanted to be heard. "I say we ride out of here. Find the whites and punish them for their dishonor."

"You speak well, Alchise," Red Head complimented him. "Would you ride at my left side?"

Surprise at this honor showed on Alchise's face. "I'd be most favored to do so, Dos-Tan-Nanta. Who else will come with us?"

"I will!"

"And I."

"I—I—I—I!" became a chorus.

Shortly after sundown, fifteen Apache braves, led by Red Head, gathered up horses and quietly departed from the San Carlos reservation. They had but a short distance to cover to find the first of the round-white-eyes they sought to punish.

Situated near a large, ancient cottonwood, in a verdant valley beside a year 'round stream, the stout, comfortable home of Gideon Chase had stood for eleven years. Two of his three children had been born here. His horse herd had increased satisfactorily and he made regular bi-annual sales to the Butterfield Stage Line and to the Army Remount Service. He also had a growing number of scruffy, starveling cattle. The agent at San Carlos had recently been purchasing some of these. Replacements, he'd told Gideon Chase, for animals missing or dead in the allotment provided the Apaches.

Gideon had no way of knowing that the plumpest and best of the cattle purchased elsewhere and driven to the agency were being held back for the agent's profit, while the tough, stringy scrub-eaters from Gideon's place served for food among the Indians. Gideon and his eldest child, a boy of fourteen, had labored until long after sundown to complete a new corral behind the low barn. As he and the youngster approached the house Gideon could identify the savory odors that indicated his wife had prepared a stew.

Rachel Chase had provided ample for her family. She knew that her man and young Rob would be starving. Bethanny, at eleven, and Samuel eight could consume man-sized portions without need of encouragement. Rachel had fixed cornbread, too, in a large cast iron skillet atop the stove. They had honey for it, from the bee tree Samuel had discovered a week past, and sand plum jam. Her garden, irrigated by water from the stream, provided lettuce, radishes and slim shoots of onion, which she combined into a salad. When the door to the cabin opened, Rachel looked up expectantly to greet her husband.

Then she screamed at the sight of Alchise's large, flat, walnut-brown face. Startled at her chore of setting table, Bethanny screamed also as five Apaches shouldered into the room. From outside she heard a belated shout of alarm. Then came the twang of a bowstring.

Rob Chase shrieked shrilly when the arrow bit into his abdomen. The hard, flat muscles parted and the obsidian tip sliced into softer tissue behind them. Fire kindled in the boy's belly and he gagged reflexively as he sank to his knees. Three more arrows struck Rob's body before he pitched onto his face. Beside him, Gideon Chase swung his rifle to the ready, yelling in an attempt to warn his wife and other children.

Fire and smoke exploded from the muzzle of Gideon's Sharps. The fat, hot slug sped toward the indistinct shape of an Apache warrior. One of the killers of Gideon's son, he grunted at the impact and dropped his bow. By then Gideon had inserted another cartridge in the chamber and fired at another brave. An arrow caught cloth in Gideon's armpit and dangled there. Another struck flesh. Hardly feeling it from the rush of adrenalin, Gideon triggered a third round. A death-moaning projectile struck the receiver of Gideon's rifle and bounced off a moment before a leaf-bladed Apache lance pierced his ribcage and ripped through lung tissue and burst his heart. Dimly, as he sank to the ground, Gideon wondered how the others in his family fared.

Inside, little Sammy launched himself at one Apache, his mother's favorite butcher knife in his right hand. He slashed a deep gouge across the warrior's left triceps muscle before being smashed away by a solid, open-handed blow. Sammy sprawled on the floor in a daze. His eyes blinked as he recognized the blur of a descending lance point. He writhed on the floor when the metal blade entered his belly and died with only a whimper.

"The women," Blunt Knife suggested, advancing on Rachel.

Rachel shrank back to the cookstove. She thought fast and snatched up the crook-necked·shank of cast iron and fitted the T-cross tooth into a stove lid. With a solid yank, she pulled it from the stove top and hurled it at the advancing Indian. Instinctively the Apache reached out with both hands to grab it before the heavy metal disc could strike him. Then he howled in agony as the fire-hot metal cooked the flesh from his fingers. Two other braves grabbed Bethanny.

Swiftly they ripped the clothes from her body. Tears streamed down her sweet, young face, distorted now by terror. Before Rachel's horrified eyes, the Apaches threw the naked girl to the floor. Bethanny screamed in terror.

A knife flashed before Rachel's eyes and then an explosion of pain jolted her chest. Not a fatal wound, for the Apaches had other ideas of how to use her body, it numbed Rachel and she sagged in the iron grip of two warriors. Immediately another yanked at her dress, ripping the bodice. Dimly she heard Bethanny scream over and over as the savages ravaged her flesh. Life ebbed from Rachel's side in a warm, wet flow. When it at last ended, with she and her daughter dead, the Apaches sniffed appreciatively of the simmering food and made gestures of pleasure and hunger.

"Eat," Red Head commanded from the door.

Some used their fingers, others large spoons to lift stew from bowls to their lips. Red Head smacked his lips in satisfaction.

"Already the gods favor our raid. We do not burn this place when we go," he commanded. "There's no reason to give the white-eyes warning."

CHAPTER 2

Clear, sharp bugle notes shivered the sky over Camp Thomas at an unusual hour. The trumpeter, Corporal Harvey, played the familiar tune of *Assembly* exactly as he had done in the pale pink and yellow light of sunrise. Disturbed at their breakfast, the men came grumbling from the mess hall.

"I tell ya I saw it with my own eyes. There was unshod pony prints, an' arrahs stuck in poor Rob an' his pappy. It's th' gawdamn' Apaches, broke out and on the rampage again," a crusty old prospector jawed on as he and Major Hampstead came from the headquarters building.

Eli Holten had broken off his morning repast at the sound of the bugle and hurried to the center of activity. To his surprise, he had not been granted admittance to the acting camp commander's office. He waited impatiently on the porch and stepped forward when the CO and his two troop officers came out with the old-timer.

"We'll dispatch two patrols, one from each troop. Two platoons each," Major Hampstead snapped out. "Chances are they'll head for Mexico. But then again, they might not."

"I'll have my Apache scouts ready to move out in five minutes, sir," Eli Holten informed the major.

21

"It won't be necessary, Holten, thank you all the same. Captain Gatewood's scouts will do quite nicely."

"Sir, I thought with two patrols going out . . ." Holten began, anxious to see some action.

"Mr. Holten, I thought I made it perfectly clear," Hampstead interrupted. "Your services are definitely *not wanted,*" he coldly added.

Stung, Holten bit back a sharp retort. "I . . . see, sir. Well, then, there is another matter which has continued for lack of attention. The young woman, Señorita Escobar, who was rescued last fall. If I'm not needed here, perhaps now would be a good time to arrange for her return to her home in Sonora?"

"Yes—yes, Holten," Maj. Hampstead said absently. "Anything you can find to do . . ."

To keep you out of our hair, Eli finished bitterly in his mind as Hampstead and his subordinates turned away to confront the troops. Already the scout began his planning. He could make it to Globe by noon the next day. Give a day or two to arrange for a wagon, some time to get his Apache scouts ready, then off to Mexico. That would solve two problems.

Any surprise visit would have been welcomed by the slender, child-faced Esmeralda Escobar. One by Eli Holten set her to unlady-like running and squeals of delight. She jumped into his arms and bussed him warmly on both cheeks, then — since they were out of doors in public view — shyly and chastely on the lips. Her full, womanly figure did not reveal itself in clothing and she appeared even younger than her nineteen years. With Eli's arrival, her faintly olive complexion glowed with new life.

"What is this, the army doesn't want you?" she

22

chided lightly, unable to disguise her pleasure at this new turn of circumstance. "I do, whether they do or not."

Inside, when he could still her babble of words, Eli broached the subject which had brought him there. "Esmeralda, time is going by for you rather faster than you seem to imagine. Also, this campaign of General Crook's appears to be developing into an extended field operation which will occupy most of my time for what will likely be months. In light of that, don't you think it would be better if you were at home, with your family?"

"No!" Esmeralda shouted. "You know I cannot go there. I'm disgraced, a common trull in their eyes. I can never show my face there again."

"Not so. No one there knows. You needn't tell them," Eli protested.

"Oh, you men. So easily deluded if your heart is set upon something. Perhaps my father, my brothers would not know, provided no one told them. But the women? Women can sense such things. I know. I am, after all, one of them. My shame would soon be known all over the *estancia*. And after that, the whole of the valley. And beyond. No. I won't go."

Holten shook his head. "I think you must, Esmeralda." The next moment he ducked a clay cup she threw at him.

It shattered on the wall and fell in reddish shards. Another followed. "No—no—no! Never will I see Sonora again! You are cruel, a beast. Don't you love me, Eli?"

"Of course I . . . Esmeralda, that has nothing to do with it. It's your welfare I'm thinking of."

"*¡Burro! ¡Estupido!* False lover!" Each word was emphasized by a hurled piece of crockery.

Bending low, Eli beat a rapid retreat. At the small

23

picket fence that divided Esmeralda's small cottage from the roadway, another saucer whizzed past Eli's head.

"And don't come back here unless you agree to let me stay," Esmeralda concluded the violent conversation.

Win Tucker and Billy Joe Jensen had been partners for longer than either wished to recall. Win, a lanky, string bean of a man, had never been considered talkative, which might account for their long association. Short and stocky, though not inclined to fat, Billy Joe could talk the leg off a stone table. They had prospected for gold, rounded up mustangs for the Army, tried dry farming in the Yuma valley, along the banks of the Colorado, and now operated a stage station. Never successful, they had also never been failures. It gave them a sort of smug satisfaction that while others had come and gone, they could make a passable go at nearly anthing, anywhere. The stage station, it turned out, had been a goldmine is disguise.

Located on the main Butterfield line between El Paso, Texas and Yuma, at the far end of the territory, their place was an overnighter. That meant revenue in the form of lodging and two meals from passengers going either direction. Three nights of the week they had a full house with two coaches pulled in for the rest. Win and Billy Joe had remodeled the sprawling one story adobe and added a second floor over the dormitory portion. They had put an awning of woven fan palm leaves over the open portion above and set up a bar, serviced through a trap door to downstairs. Tables and chairs adorned a platform constructed over the roof and on the busiest nights the outdoor cantina became a popular place.

Arizona's desert never lacked for thirsty folks, whether it be tea, cooled in a clay olla, or pop-skull from a questionable barrel. Win and Billy Joe provided all these delights. And Manuel, their wrangler, could do about any tune on his guitar, provided someone could hum a few bars to him. Before long the stage station became the social center of that desolate portion of the territory. It happened to be an off night when Dos-Tan-Nanta and his reservation jumpers paid a visit.

Horses whinnied nervously and stamped the ground in the corral. The five passengers, and two crew sat on the rooftop listening to Manuel play soulful Mexican ballads. Billy Joe tended bar and Win rustled food down below. The discomfited animals grew louder and Manuel excused himself to investigate. He had hardly been gone two minutes when an eerie scream filled the night. A man and his wife, passengers, exchanged worried looks. A traveling salesman for a harness company rose, along with Fred, the shotgun guard, and went to fetch their weapons. Before they returned flaming torches flickered in the darkness like bloated fire flys.

"Eeeeiiii-i-i-i-! Ki-ki-ki-yiiii!" shrill voices came out of the night.

"My word, what was that?" the bookish husband asked.

"Dear, you don't think it's Indians, do you?" his pinched-faced wife wailed.

"It's gawdamned 'Pachies, is what that is," Billy Joe declared, blowing out the lantern which illuminated the bar where he worked. From under the counter he produced a sixgun and a ten gauge Parker shotgun. Two boxes of shells followed. "Folks you got about thirty seconds to get securely in your rooms or arm yourselves and help fight for your lives."

Billy Joe missed by only a fraction of a second. In less than thirty-one seconds the first arrow thudded into the boards of the roof-top saloon. Ten more followed. Then a flaming brand followed. Sloshing it with a pitcher of lemonade, another of the passengers extinguished the blaze before real harm was done.

"What about your man, Manuel?" a leather-faced rancher asked.

"Won't be hearin' from him again," Billy Joe opined. "That scream was the heathen 'Paches cuttin off his balls I reckon."

Scrabbling sounds drew their attention to the parapet of the outer wall on the west side. A long-haired Apache head appeared over the top. Billy Joe blew it away to the eyebrows with a load of No. 2 goose shot. He opened the breech and replaced the smoking casing with a fresh load of double O. The sound of splintering wood came from below.

Shots followed and then a brief scream. Voices speaking Apache raised a shout. Footsteps, padded by moccasins, sounded on the stairs. Another shower of arrows found mark in flesh as the coach driver grunted and dropped his sixgun. He bent to retrieve it when the first Apache burst onto the roof from the stairway. The warrior mouthed an Apache obscenity and fired a rusty old trade rifle at Billy Joe.

The Apache never saw his miss. Fred blew him in half with a double barrel blast of 00 buck from his sawed-off coach gun. The frightened woman screamed from the window of their room while her husband tried ineffectually to bring fire on the attackers with his small pocket pistol. Shotguns and six-shooters belched flame around the platform.

Glass shattered behind the bar. More Apaches poured into the battle. The night went orange-bright with a final detonation from Billy Joe's Parker and a warrior flopped dead on the plank floor, his head entirely pulverized by lead pellets. A shrill scream followed. Then the crash of a door being ripped open.

"No!" the foppish husband bellowed. "Oh, God, no!"

Then all protests turned to shrieks and groans and the soft, gutteral laughter of the victorious Apaches.

Not one to be bossed, or outshouted by a woman, Eli set off at once to visit General Crook in the field. The general had last been reported headed toward the border with New Mexico, in the Douglas area. Four days hard riding brought Eli within distance of Crook's patrols. From a somewhat reluctant Capt. John Bourke, Eli learned the location of Crook's headquarters and reached there in mid-morning the next day.

"General, we've got two problems," the scout presented with scant preamble of amenities. "First off it seems everyone and his brother knows why you left me at Camp Thompson. The officers and gentlemen in charge there made it clear to me that neither my opinions nor my face were welcome. I can't do you any good if I can't observe them from inside."

"Granted that," Crook said gruffly. His shaggy mane of graying hair stood out under the brim of the English pith helmet he affected in the field. "Very well, I'll relieve you of that duty. What else?"

"There's a young woman who is almost a year overdue in being returned to her family."

"Ah, yes, the Escobar woman. I presume your presence here has something to do with that, also?"

"Yes, General. I would like your permission, with appropriate orders cut, to escort Señorita Escobar back to her father's ranch in Sonora. They are, I understand, quite wealthy. From what I've seen of this Apache problem, it wouldn't hurt to have a friend at court, so to speak, for future dealings with Mexico."

"Hummmm. You've posed me quite a puzzler, Mr. Holten," Crook responded after a short pause. "I need you here, yet I'm damned to know what to do with you. On the other hand, our rescue of Miss Escobar, and her safe return to her family, would, as you say, generate a certain atmosphere of gratitude. That could be valuable. It could also bring down the diplomatic wrath of the Mexican government on us if it were done with all the trappings of an official military act of courtesy."

"I figured to do it with the Apache Kid and my other scouts, if you'll agree to that, sir," Holten offered.

"Umm. Won't do. You're aware, I'm sure, that the Apaches are not looked upon with favor by the populace. The Mexicans in particular have a deep distrust, suspicion and fear of the Apaches. If you show up down there with half a dozen Apaches, you'll either not get any assistance when needed, or the Federales would scoop you up as a renegade and execute you along with the scouts. Likewise, they would be, of necessity, in uniform if under orders, and that would violate the Treaty of Guerrero, which keeps us on this side of the border."

Unable to find an argument that would counter the general's logic, Holten decided to withdraw gracefully. "You've got me there, General. At least I can have the Kid and four of my scouts accompany us to the border and wait there for my return?"

Crook nodded absently, reaching for his coffee cup. "That you can do, but not one foot into Mexico, understand."

"Yes, sir."

"When will you leave, Mr. Holten?"

"Soon as I can round up some men to go along. Three, four days, no more than a week."

"God go with you, then," Crook dismissed him.

CHAPTER 3

Humming their dull, monotone salutation, a cloud of gnats undulated through the rising heat thermals on the high desert plateau. Far off, a green and purple haze marked the location of Globe, Arizona Territory, at an even higher elevation. The spherical cluster of tiny insects found the man and horse delightful distractions from their fruitless hovering. They swarmed into eyes, ears, nose and mouths. Seeking moisture, they also seemed to enjoy the torment they brought.

Eli Holten cursed them roundly and swatted with his hat. What, he tried to recall, was that saying about Englishmen and the noonday sun? A good twenty-five miles yet to go and at a walk because of the heat. He'd not see the cool comfort of Esmeralda's small house until the next day.

As it happened, he didn't see it then. Esmeralda refused to grant him admission. She called him a bully and a cad for wanting to send her away. She insisted that he change his mind before she granted him the comforts of her home. Eli decided that the only way to get on with it would be to quickly round up five or six men capable of facing the hazards the journey might promise. Then to proceed to Sonora, protests from Esmeralda or no. The place to find such men, he concluded, would be the Champion.

Globe's premier saloon, the Champion Billiard Hall and Saloon, occupied a prestigeous location at the corner of Broadway and Push Street. There the civic leaders met to discuss the doings of the day and imbibe of the "finest wines, liquors and cigars to be found in the territory," as the sign outside advertised. Generally they held forth at the bar. When the coarser element, the ones of interest to Eli Holten, assembled, the gentlemen of Globe retired to the "Wine Room" at the rear. Eli found the establishment disappointingly empty when he entered shortly after the noon hour.

"What'll it be, Mr. Holten?" the apron inquired of the familiar customer.

"A beer, Felix," Eli informed the small statured half-owner of the Champion.

While he sipped his brew, Eli looked around the adobe structure and at the white muslin ceiling cloth that protected the customers from the ever-present scorpions and centipedes that inhabited such structures. Everything on the desert, animal or vegetable, bit or stung, Eli reflected. And most of them were poisonous. For a moment he wished longingly for the relatively hospitable nature of Dakota Territory. Several men entered, one of whom Eli recognized. After he ordered a drink, Eli spoke to him.

"Barleycorn, if you have a minute, I've got something I'd like to talk about with you."

"Ah, sure, Holten." Slight of stature, Barleycorn John Oates ambled over to where Eli sat at a small table. He doffed his low-crown, brown hat with the turquoise and silver band and straddled a chair. "What's on your mind?"

"I've a little job to do and I think you might be interested," Eli told him.

The scout took in the loose tan, square-cut shirt, worn outside Oates' rust-colored whipcord trousers. Navajo moccasins and an abundance of flashy Navajo jewelry gave the five foot seven, former stagecoach guard an air of a man gone "native." It was hard to believe, Holten considered, that John Oates had lived but a few years over twenty. His face was seamed and creased by long exposure to the sun, and his faded blue eyes seemed watery. Eli made note that despite his bibulous sobriquet, Barleycorn John Oates held a glass of goat's milk. Men in the past who had considered the tee-totaler's mode of dress and choice of drinks to imply an effeminate nature learned the hard way what a terrible mistake they had made.

To the contrary, Eli Holten considered him sound and an ideal choice for the trip to Esmeralda's home. He felt no offense when the first question Oates asked was how much the job paid.

"The satisfaction of doing a good turn," Eli responded. "And twenty dollars gold."

"Twenty dollars! Hell, that's hardly the price of all night with a good woman."

"That's base pay," Holten emphasized. "What we'll do is escort Señorita Esmeralda Escobar back to her family in Sonora. Her father is a rich *haciendado*, and will no doubt reward us lavishly for her safe return. Even if he doesn't, you're not out everything. You'll still have my twenty dollars in gold."

Barleycorn John cocked an eyebrow. "Sonora, you say? There's Apaches, and Yaquis, and bandits, and God knows what running wild down there. We go through *them* for a lousy twenty dollars?"

"You're not afraid, are you, John?" the scout prodded.

"Better be certain right now that's not the case,"

33

Oates growled. "Only thing I was wondering is how many of us are going and how much ammunition are we packin'?"

Eli smiled. "That's better. I reckoned on taking . . . oh, say six of you and myself. Along with Señorita Escobar."

"Seven of us? Just seven of us against . . . all that?" Oates returned, gesturing with a wild sweep of his arm to encompass all of the far distant state of Sonora, Mexico.

"I'd figured to take along my Apache scouts, but General Crook said no. You happen to know of any other fellers who might be interested?"

"I ain't said *I'm* interested as yet. But you might try Ed Hendrickson. He's due back from Show-Low tomorrow. Seven of us," Oates repeated wonderingly. "If we made it, got away clean, it'd sure be magnificent, wouldn't it?"

"Let me talk to Ed, then. I'll consider you in, until I hear otherwise," Eli responded, unwilling to admit to the difficulty of what he proposed.

By nightfall, Esmeralda had changed her tactics. Still adamant about not leaving Globe and Eli's attentions, she decided to turn on all her feminine wiles to convince him to keep her on as his mistress. When he appeared on her doorstep, she all but dragged him inside and directly to bed.

"Oh, Eli, I missed you so while you were gone," she declared in a melting tone. Arms flung around his neck, though she had to stretch to do so, the raven-haired beauty used her weight to pull the scout inside.

"I will say that's a rather warmer greeting than I received this morning," Eli allowed as he attempted

34

not to stumble.

Esmeralda affected a pout. "I've been mean and petty, Eli, and I'm sorry."

"That means you'll reconsider going back to your family?" he asked hopefully.

"Well . . ." she evaded. "That means I want you to know how much you mean to me."

While Eli tried to separate the meaning of the "means" in her convoluted sentence, Esmeralda took him by the hand and coaxed him toward the bed. It didn't take much effort. It had been a long, lonely two weeks since they had last been together. Eli felt himself rising to the occasion as they neared that article of furniture which had supported so much of their pleasure in the past.

Recalling that, Eli took Esmeralda in his arms. They kissed tenderly, the contact lacking all the fires of passion that earlier embraces had generated. Both of them soon rectified that. With exploring hands and tongues they soon kindled a rebirth of erotic eagerness. Esmeralda ground her pelvis against Eli's iron-hard frame. Gasping she pulled her lips away.

"Oooh, Eli. You're so—so manly."

"What I am is all fussed up. I missed you while I was gone."

"And I you. Hurry, dearest, *caro mio*, get out of those smelly buckskins and let me see your marvelous body."

Eli eased them onto the bed. All thoughts of go or stay had left his mind as well as hers. Their night became one of greater ecstasy than either had experienced in a long while.

After a breakfast of ham, grits, biscuits and eggs, Eli left with the kisses of his thanks on her lips.

*   *   *

"I'm Ed Hendrickson. Hear you're lookin' for me," a tall, lean man, who out-reached Eli Holten by two inches, Ed had cool green eyes, studded with flecks of brown, which seemed to stare beyond the horizon one moment and plunge into one's head the next. He extended a ham-like hand for Eli to grasp.

"Eli Holten. I'm on leave from General Crooks headquarters. I've got a little errand to perform, sort of on the behest of the territory. A young lady we rescued from the Apaches last fall is in need of protection and transportation back to her home in Sonora."

"Mezkin, eh? Might be we could be in for some trouble mixin' in where none want us," Ed opined.

"On a mission of mercy? Ed, we stand to be well rewarded by her father. He's a *hacien—haciendada*, if that's the right word. We'll have my Apache scouts as escort to the border. Then a four or five day ride to the ranch. Barleycorn Oates is signin' on. How about you?"

Hendrickson's handsome face split in a grin. "I've never been known to turn my back on a tough job. What's the rest of it?"

Eli explained, including the twenty dollar base pay. Ed nodded at that. "Good idea," he agreed. "That way no one can complain they didn't get something for their troubles. I like that. Count me in."

That night Eli sat down to a remarkable meal, savory and cooked to perfection. In bed, Esmeralda became a wildcat. The tortured squawking of the bed frame could be clearly heard outside the small adobe house.

"Oooh! Ayeee, Eli, harder, faster, ayyyyyeeee!" she

36

keened over and over.

Inexhaustable, Esmeralda kept Eli in a state of excitement until his belly muscles cramped and his legs refused to support him when he rose to get a glass of water. When he fell back on the bed, Esmeralda came at him again.

By morning, in spite of two hours of sleep, Eli could barely walk.

"Twenty dollars! Sure an' yer full o' *mierda,* if ye think anyone would work for so paltry a sum," Carlos Brian O'Banyon exploded.

Seated at a table in front of the irate Irish-Mexican, Eli Holten eyed him icily. He had heard vaguely of Carlos O'Banyon. Tough and cocky, he was noted more for his skill as a cook than as a gunhand. He wore a Merwin and Hulbert revolver tucked in his waistband, his trousers upheld by a length of rope. His white, cotton peasant shirt Eli attributed more to his culinary profession than to poverty. O'Banyon wore enough chains of Mexican gold and thick medallions to various saints around his neck to provide a family of five a comfortable life for several years. He could be a real asset to the expedition, Eli decided. Yet, not if the spirited bantam thought he had in the least any command of the situation.

"Mr. O'Banyon, before you tell another man he is full of shit, I suggest you determine in advance that he is incapable of picking you up in his bare hands and snapping you in half with a flick of his wrists," Eli grated out like ice breaking on the Mississippi. "Something I am about to do if I don't hear an abject apology at once."

O'Banyon blinked. Then a beautiful smile spread on his round, copper-hued face. "Ah, sure an' me tongue got in the way o' me reason there, Mr. Holten," he obligingly burbled. "'Twas one o' them things an' no insult intended."

"And cut the County Cork blarney, O'Banyon. You speak better Spanish and Apache than English from what I hear."

Affecting a deeply grieved expression, Carlos O'Banyon wrung his hat in his hands. "I confess, you've found me out. It's my mother's doing that I speak the tongue of Iberia. My father, bless his soul, was the very heart of an Irishman. Between them I grew up grandly confused."

"I imagine so. Are you too dithered to properly handle that hogleg you've got stuck in a place that threatens your finer attributes?"

"The Merwin and Hulbert you mean? By your leave if you wish to step outside I will gladly show you the superior range of this fine piece of machinery. It was made, as I'm sure you know, for the Army, though it does well on civilian fodder."

"I'm always in the mood for a shooting demonstration," Eli allowed. "We'll go out back."

On the way, Eli stopped to retrieve a dozen empty bottles from a supply kept in a barrel by the rear door. Outside, the hill behind the Champion sparkled brightly in the sun, as though invested with a myriad of precious jewels. Others had contested their skill and left a glittering display of their marksmanship. An urchin of about ten years, obviously hiding out from chores at home, lounged against the wall of a storage shed. Eli motioned him over.

"Take these bottles up on that hill to extreme revolver range. There's a ten cent piece in it for you."

"Like hell," the cocky little brat piped back. "Most folks give me a nickle apiece."

Impatient at such ill manners in a child, Eli bent

down close to the freckle-faced waif. "How'd you like your ears boxed?"

Hands fisted on hips, the red-headed youngster impudently looked Eli up and down. "How'd you like a kick in the balls?"

In a blur, Eli's left hand lashed out and wound the boy's shirtfront into a ball. Without visible effort the scout yanked the lad off his feet. "I kind of like a spunky kid," Eli growled, his lips only inches from the button nose. "But if you keep up the the back-talk, you'll never see your next birthday."

Face suddenly ashen, the boy stammered a reply. "Y-Y-Yesssir. Two cents a bottle's the goin' rate and I even rake up the shards."

Laughing, Eli set him down and gave him a swat on the bottom. "Get on with it, then. And I'll make it three cents for a good job."

Carlos proved to have more than a facile tongue. With almost casual ease he blasted apart the widely spaced bottles, reloaded and repeated the demonstration on six more. Sensing the implied challenge, Eli drew his Remington and exterminated the narrow neck segments left standing amid the slivers of glass.

"Wowie, mister," the urchin said with awe. "You're somethin' with that iron."

"You ought to see what I can do to charging Sioux warriors, shootin' under the belly of my galloping horse," Eli teased, laughing inwardly at the ridiculous image he had created.

The boy inserted his right index finger in his mouth and nibbled at a well-gnawed fingernail. "Not much, I bet. My Paw says a man can't hit shit from a runnin' horse."

Caught in his own spoof, Eli could only growl. "There you go with that outhouse mouth of yours again. Seems to me a good wash'in with a bar of lye soap might be in order."

"Not me, you don't," the boy blurted out, poised to run. "Ain't no soap ever gonna touch me. Swimmin' in the tanks is enough to get off the stink."

Eli flipped him a half dollar. "Here you go. Keep the change."

"Thaa-ank you, Mister," the kid gulped and took off at a dead run for the candy jars at the general mercantile.

"You'll do," Eli addressed to O'Banyon, who had bent over with laughter. "Are you in, O'Banyon?"

"You can put my promise in the bank. Nothin' else doin', so I guess I'll go."

"Good. Ed Hendrickson and Barleycorn Oates are signed up already."

"Foine, foine. When do we leave?"

"I'll let you know on that. Just keep around close."

CHAPTER 4

Night birds sang of sweet romance, while crickets provided the orchestra. The dulcet bouquet of heady pines perfumed the bedroom of Esmeralda Escobar's house on the edge of Globe. Two naked figures lay sprawled in positions of replete satisfaction. Esmeralda's heart pounded with a patent belief in her victory. Eli Holten ached from the exertions of no less than seven bouts in the fields of love.

Feeling more vanquished than victor, he shuddered at the feather-light touch of Esmeralda's fingers on his exhausted flesh. Eli groaned.

For the past five days, or nights rather, he had been given an amorous feast unlike any man, save the fabled potentates of the East, had ever experienced. Esmeralda had literally drained him dry. At times, Eli wondered if Esmeralda was seeking revenge by humping him to death. . .

"I hear you're lookin for some men to escort a wagon?" a squeaky voice assailed Eli Holten's ears.

Eli looked up from the stout mug of coffee he nursed at a table in the Champion. He saw a gangling youth, all elbows and knees, with a mop of cottony hair, big china blue eyes and the pale, gold freckles of childhood on his sun-browned pug nose.

A cheap whiskey hangover could not have tormented Eli any more than the aftermath of his night of amorous excess.

"The operative word is *men,* Sonny," Eli growled.

Showing his affront, the boy replied, "I'm nineteen."

More likely fourteen or fifteen, Eli mentally evaluated. No matter the near six foot height. "What do you do, sonny?"

"M'name's not sonny, it's Peter Taylor. And I'm the best hoss wrangler in these parts."

"Are you now? By who's lights?" Eli queried.

"I've worked two sum—ah—years for Butterfield. Breakin' and then tendin' teams," Peter defended.

"How good are you with a gun?" Eli demanded.

Peter's face fell slightly. "Not as good as I am with horses. What's that got to do with it?"

"I'm headed for the south of Sonora. I'm told there's more Apaches and bandits between here and where we're going than anything else but rocks and cactus. Gunhandling's an important part of the qualifications."

A ray of hope shone in Peter's eyes. "I can hit what I shoot at."

Eli considered it a moment. "There's lots who can't. I'll give it some thought. If there's no one else signs on, I'll give you the benefit of the doubt."

"Thank you kindly. But you're makin' a mistake if you don't take me along as wrangler," Peter concluded confidently.

Over the next hour, Eli turned down Oscar Rodriguez, a manish-dressed Sadie Hawks, and three trail bums who only mumbled their names. He took on Luke Walker because of his family reputation. Luke's grandfather had been Captain Walker of the

42

Texas Rangers, the man who recommended modifications and additions that made Colt's first workable sixgun into a practical firearm. Try as he might, Eli could find no one else suitable. And time was drawing short.

Elijah Dantz and Karl Richter had been partners since they skipped grade school classes together. Somewhere along the line they had turned to prospecting without really knowing how or why. They had their successes and their failures. Through it all their friendship became a bond closer than between brothers. When one of their consistently below standard strikes would play out, they would move on to another without argument or accusations. When they found a truly rich pocket in as unlikely a spot as Skull Canyon, a place sacred to the Apaches, they agreed to keep it secret and not file on the claim.

It worked to their advantage, for no one knew where they found their gold. Attempts to follow them failed as the wiley pair misled their pursuers through a desolate and waterless area, then over a lava bed and into twisting, steep-walled canyons, always further away from the true location, until the gold-hungry surveillants gave up or perished from the desert's privations. Only sharp and knowing Apache eyes spied them out.

"They take the yellow metal from our sacred mountain," Alchise informed Dos-Tan-Nanta. "Two men, four horses and four burros. They are alone and leave all other white-eyes behind."

Red Head considered the report and nodded. "They must be punished for defiling the dying place of our ancestors. Where do they make their camp?"

"It's by the tall pinnacle the whites call the Needle's Eye."

"Tonight, then, we move into place," Dos-Tan-Nanta commanded.

Dawn found Lije and Karl in a philosophical mood over coffee and a breakfast of beans, fatback, and hardtack soaked and fried in bacon grease. The purple shades of night retreated behind the high canyon walls to the west and pastel blue, pale pink and an intense white lit up the opposite horizon. Karl, his words thick with German accent, offered an out of the ordinary proposition

"Vhat happens ven ve are gone from here?"

"How do you mean, Karl?" Lije asked.

"Vhen ve are det. Ve haf not filed on dis claim. It will become lost, *nein?*"

"Well, ah, I suppose so. Once we're dead, it won't be of any use to us, right? I ain't got any kin, do you?"

Karl frowned in remembering. "Not dat I know of."

Lije's broad, Bavarian face beamed. "Then what have we to worry about.?"

He leaned forward, so that the arrow intended for his rib cage grazed the leather joint on the back of his suspenders and buried the shaft in the sandy soil. Lije upset the coffee pot as he sprang forward as though stung by a bee. Recovering his balance he whirled about, looking into the near distance.

"What the hell was that?" he asked.

Karl sat bug-eyed, staring at the quivering fletchings of the arrow. "Iss Indians, I think," he said quietly as he reached for his rifle.

Three puffs of smoke rose from the scrub brush around the camp. Inaccurately aimed, the slugs created plumes of dust where they struck the ground. A dozen arrows followed, along with two Apache

44

lances. Karl cried out when a feathered projectile drove into his left thigh. He lost his footing and rolled to one side. Still the doughty pair had seen nothing to shoot at.

"We've got to get out of the open," Elijah suggested.

"Der mine," Karl offered. At once he began to crawl toward the entrance.

Elijah turned about and fired blindly at their enemy, then ran ahead to provide more cover so Karl could make it. He stuffed fresh cartridges through the loading gate of his Winchester, eyes scanning the low paloverde trees and salt bush. A gray-green sage wriggled and seemingly out of nowhere an Apache warrior raised up. Elijah knocked him back down with two rapid .44 rounds. Panting with the effort, Karl reached the mine. He took up the covering fire while Elijah went further into their drift and wheeled forward a crude, handmade, wooden mine car. With this they blocked the entrance.

"We've got water," Elijah observed, pointing to two barrels attached to support beams.

"But no food and little ammunition," Karl responded.

Bullets smacked into the thick end planks of the ore car. Karl and Lije exchanged desperate looks. Both positioned themselves and brought down two incautious Apaches over the next twenty minutes. The siege lasted most of the day. At last Red Head sent three men around and above the mine entrance. They made bundles of still green branches, including pungent sage and paloverde. These they ignited and threw, blazing, through the entrance. Eyes smarting and chests heaving from the smoke, Elijah and Karl staggered out of the confines of their mine, into the eager hands of the Apaches.

After they had noisily rendered up their souls to satisfy the Apaches gods, Dos-Tan-Nanta and Alchise spoke together, along with a recent arrival, Three Fingers, who came from San Carlos with nine fresh men. Their conversation centered upon the future.

"We must go into Mexico," Three Fingers urged.

"What if we don't?" Red Head posed. "The soldier-chief, Crook, will expect us to do that. Patrols will be heavy."

"Dos-Tan-Nanta has a point," Alchise approved.

"Then what is there for us to profit from if we stay here?" Three Fingers inquired.

"There is a *pen-dik-olye* village at the place of Sunset Rock, which the whites call Hobart. It is small. Few men are there to protect the women and children. There's many horses and much firewater. Mescal, tequila, *quisbah*. We can take what we want."

Three Fingers' eyes narrowed. "You're sure of this?"

"I am," Red Head answered confidently. "We can be there in three days ride if we move slowly."

"Will the whites expect us?" Three Fingers pressed.

"Not if we don't tell them we're coming," Alchise quipped.

Eli Holten had taken care in selecting a wagon. It had thick walls and floor planks, oversized axles and stout, fat spokes. Steel tires, shrunk tight, insured long life for the wheels. The hubs had been heavily lubricated and a large pail of dark amber axle grease hung from a hook on one side. A complete duplicate set of tongue, single and double trees, along with the

46

steel concentric circles of the front running gear had been lashed under the bed. Four handsome mules pulled the vehicle. A matched twosome of ginger and roan, the other pair grays with black muzzles, ear tips and spotted rumps. They had been sold to Eli with the assurance that the quartet were of exemplary temperment.

When it came time to hook them up, their fractious behavior quickly caused the scout to doubt the truthfulness of the livestock broker. One jenny nipped constantly, another stood stubborn and still and kicked the dashboard of the wagon repeatedly. A third refused to move at all. Holten was about ready to do serious murder when Peter Taylor showed up in the cool dawn light.

"You're not doing it right," the youthful would-be adventurer declared. "Here, let me give it a try."

"What—?" Eli managed.

Peter didn't wait for approval, but went to the rebellious foursome. "Here now, you shouldn't be doing that," he crooned to the kicker. "You're not a wheeler anyway, are you? Come on take this one's place."

One by one Peter rearranged the mules, the grays to the rear, on opposite sides than Eli had placed them, the brindles leading. Not once did he get a nip, nor did the stubborn one balk in the least when led by Peter to the traces. When the harnessing had been completed, Peter turned to the rough-edged assembly.

"That Morgan you've got looks like he'll make the distance," Peter observed of Eli's Sonny, hands on hips, head canted to the right in a gesture of critical study. "From the way the rest appear, you'd all do well to consider taking remounts. I gather the lady will ride on the wagon?" Peter concluded with a nod to a young woman standing near Ed Hendrickson.

"She will," Holten informed the youth. "She's not the one we're to escort. She's a friend of Ed Hendrickson."

"How do," Joan Wallis offered indifferently.

"I'm just fine, ma'am," Peter returned. He blushed slightly as he tipped his hat.

"That display with the mules," Eli injected, "has changed my mind. You're hired on as our wrangler. Do you have a gun with you?"

Peter's flash of pink turned to a deep scarlet. "Uh—no, sir. I, ah, have to buy one."

"Get to it, then. We want to get away from here before the sun's too hot," Eli commanded.

Swelled with pride in his acceptance, Peter set off for the Champion, intent on picking up a bargain some stranger had left in pawn to cover his debts. Ed Hendrickson assisted Joan Wallis aboard the wagon. She expertly hefted the reins and clucked the mules into motion. When the little cavalcade reached Esmeralda Escobar's house, another rebellion developed immediately.

"No-no-no-no! I will not go. You can't make me. I want to stay here," Esmeralda shrieked at Eli, desperate now her plan had obviously failed.

"Esmeralda, sweetheart, listen to me," Eli pleaded. "I checked this with Judge Bush when he came over from Prescott. Even in this country you cannot be legally in charge of your affairs for another two years. You are only nineteen. And, as a citizen of Mexico, their laws apply also. You must return to your father until you reach your majority. Or until you are married."

"There! You see? If you had married me, like I said, none of this would have happened. You are a beast. You've grown tired of me and want a new woman, no? You are heartless, cruel." Tears came and Esmeralda began to beat on Eli's chest with her tiny fists.

Bedevilled out of his scant diplomacy, Eli simply lifted Esmeralda into his arms and carried her to the wagon box. "Ed, Barleycorn, Carlos, inside and gather her belongings," he commanded.

"You monster! Son of the devil! I'll—I'll never speak to you again," Esmeralda wailed.

"If that's a promise, I'll let you sit on the seat. Otherwise you can stay in the back with your clothes and belongings," Eli snapped, patience entirely shattered.

Within twenty minutes the wagon had been loaded. Already aboard were staple supplies, tents and camping gear. Two packhorses carried the personal items of the rest of the company. With Esmeralda's loud complaints stringing behind, the rag-tag column departed from Globe.

CHAPTER 5

Small, fleecy puffballs rushed together as though magnetically charged and formed a single, black-bellied *cumulo nimbus*. Gathering momentum, the rain-filled cloud whisked down toward a collection of five solid buildings, clustered around a central Plaza de Armas in typical Southwest style. The beaten earth square was distinguished by the skeletal structure of a windmill, which could be seen at a far distance and promised surcease for the weary desert traveler. Three smaller dwellings, in more or less a row, marked the limits of the community and the occupants of these showed the only reaction when a single rumble of thunder announced the deluge of fat raindrops that washed over the town.

Two women rushed for clotheslines and frantically began to remove their wash. A third stopped half way and resigned herself to the inevitable. The downpour came in such volume and speed that the thumb-thick droplets shattered on the desert hard-pan sending a muddy spray to a height of six feet. It rattled on tin roofs like hail and its seething hiss reminded the town's occupants of a steam boiler. In an instant the world turned gray. Mayor Jacob Klein could not see across the plaza from his general mercantile to the Empty Stirrup saloon.

Hobart, Arizona Territory consisted of two saloons, Klein's general mercantile, a harness shop and livery, and a *panaderia*, which provided savory bread, thick, flavorful tortillas, *pan dulce*, and saucer-sized sugar cookies of a deep, golden color and heavenly taste. Mayor Klein wished they had other enterprises in the town. They needed a doctor, and perhaps a bank. A butcher shop would be nice. Yet, somehow, the mainstream of development continued to flow past Hobart in favor of other places. Klein breathed deeply of the rain-sweetened air.

He silently gave thanks for it. The brief squall would freshen the town, wash away some of the dust from building fronts and promote green and vigorous life for a short while. Desert plants would bloom and in shadowy places a little grass might appear for a day or two. Although the celestial water held considerable warmth, the wind that accompanied it had a chill edge. Mayor Klein shivered and turned back inside his store. The storm started to move on, yet it did not take with it Mayor Klein's uneasy conviction that something portentous would happen that day.

Outside of town, a quarter of a mile to the north, Dos-Tan-Nanta spoke to his men. "We'll attack behind the rain, before the white-eyes begin to stir about again."

"Already the storm moves to the East," Alchise informed the leader.

"To your horses, then," Red Head commanded. "You have more guns now. Make good use of them."

They rode in spread, wide apart. When a woman's shriek announced their presence, each warrior fired at the open windows and doorways of the buildings around the square. Their random shots did little damage, but accompanied by the shrill yipping of the dread war cry, had a tremendous effect on morale. Women squeaked or screamed, men shouted in angry defiance. At the livery, the proprietor took after the Apaches with a shotgun. He blasted one off his horse as the determined brave clawed at the rawhide thong that secured the corral gate. The warrior's companion returned fire, but the furious ex-Texan stood his ground.

Another load of buckshot peppered the Apache's shoulder and he sagged off howling. Having fired the single charge in his trade musket, a breech clouted brave slipped from his mount and came at the hostler from behind. A swift, muscular bronze arm whipped around the liveryman's throat and bent back his head. A wedge of fire pierced his back, expelling the breath of life from his lungs. The Apache stabbed again and again, demolishing the white man's right kidney, then puncturing the left one. Pouring blood, the murdered livery keeper sagged and fell away to the straw-littered floor of the stable. Whooping in delight, the Apache warrior sprinted for his horse.

Through the buildings of town the unprepared residents fought valiantly against the relentless Apaches. The twenty inhabitants of Hobart had little chance against the savage attackers. Mayor Klein cried out in alarm at the sound of the first shots and war whoops. He dived behind a heavy wooden counter of New England maple and dragged a repeating rifle off the rack on the wall behind him. Fingers trembling at the knowledge of an Apache raid, he had managed to load five and scatter seven cartridges when the glass front of his store exploded inward, propelled by an Apache on a terrified paint horse.

"You baaaastard!" Jacob Klein shouted as he came up to kneel behind the counter, resting his rifle across the glass-covered advertisement for ladies' unmentionables. He fired a round, quickly chambered another, and shot again.

Both slugs caught the Apache's horse in the chest. Powerful lungs shredded and the horse made a pitiful scream, threw its rider and crashed headlong into a rank of glass-fronted display bins. The Apache slammed broadside into a barrel of flour, breaking several ribs and rupturing the staves.

A cloud of white exploded in the store. Mayor Klein could not make out his enemy through it. He moved to his right to get a better view. A bronze arm flashed in the air and a stone axe crushed the mayor's skull. Outside the store the hooting and howling and screams of terror diminished. Aching terribly from the broken ribs, Thunder Walker limped out into the Plaza de Armas. The living women and children and wounded males had been gathered by the windmill. A wide smirk spread on Thunder Walker's face.

"Now we test their men's courage, no?" he asked Red Head.

Scar returned to the small cavalcade with important news. When the wagon and the mounted men halted, Eli Holten could hear faintly in the distance the rattle and pop of firearms. It only served to verify what the Apache scout reported.

"Reservation jumpers have attacked the white-eye village of Hobart," Scar informed Eli.

"They are many?" Eli inquired.

"More than enough," Scar answered laconically.

"Did they leave any in reserve?"

Eli's military term was well known to the scouts. "No. All are in the fight. There are women in the village, and children," Scar concluded with a knowing nod of his head.

"Then they won't be expecting a counter attack from behind," Eli speculated aloud. "Everyone ready. Joan, you and Esmeralda arm yourselves. A shotgun I would think, and revolvers. We're going after those Apaches."

"Do we have to?" Joan Wallis asked, genuine concern prompting her query.

Her yellow-brown hair hung limply in unfurled curls from under a calico bonnet. She wore a man's shirt, which only served to accent her large, firm breasts. Her hazel eyes swam with unshed tears and her usually creamy-tan complexion had turned ashen.

"They're in our way," Eli stated simply.

To those familiar with the Apache style of raiding it was answer enough. If not challenged and driven off, they would soon find the trail left by the wagon and so many horses. Emboldened by their success in Hobart, they wouldn't hesitate a moment to take on this new prize offered by providence. When Eli had seen to every member's preparations, he nodded and gestured them forward.

"We'll spread out at the last minute and rush the town," he outlined his strategy. "Lots of shooting, but I want you to make every bullet count when you have a solid target. Let them think they ran into Crook's main column."

Twenty minutes brought them within sight of the windmill. Another five raised the town. Nothing seemed to stir, though three buildings were briskly burning. Eli spread his scant force and they set off at a rapid canter, weapons at the ready.

First to spot their approach, Thunder Walker also became first of the renegades to die. His chest ripped apart inside by a bullet from Eli Holten's Winchester, he fell in a heap between the general mercantile and the Cantina Diablo. Then Eli, John Oates and Ed Hendrickson bolted out into the plaza. Weapons blazing, they were soon joined at oblique angles by Carlos O'Banyon and Peter Taylor. Sgt. Ski-Be-Nan-Ted along with Scar and the Apache scouts came from a third side. Luke Walker rode beside the wagon.

Thoroughly surprised and caught for the most part with only knives and short range hand weapons, the Apache raiders dashed for their horses. The gods had frowned on them and safety lay only in retreat. Their rapid withdrawal took them past the wagon. A shotgun boomed in the hands of Joan Wallis and an Apache's head disappeared in a crimson froth. Another howled from pellet wounds, though he remained in the saddle. In a thrice they had fled the scene. It took only seconds to determine none remained in town.

"They fled because they believe the gods have deserted them," Ski-Be-Nan-Ted, the Apache Kid, remarked.

He pointed to where a whiteman rested his back against one upright of the windmill, his arms tied behind the eight-by-eight post, head lolled to one side in the eventual release of death. He had been stripped of his clothing and a small bed of coals still smoldered between his legs where it had roasted his testicles until they exploded.

"It is believed that such tortures bring disgrace on the one who uses them. He's abandoned by his gods, who anger over these things," the Kid explained. "There's much hatred in these raiders or they would never resort to such acts."

Everywhere in the plaza Eli and his small band found evidence of torture and maiming. Several of those afflicted begged for the mercy of a quick bullet. Esmeralda, horror-stricken, approached the scout.

"I—in the years of my captivity, I came to know the Apaches to be fierce in battle, and cruel to their captives, but I never saw them commit so many terrible atrocities. Wh-who are these men to do such things?"

"I don't know, Es."

"Oh . . . oh, my . . . God!" Joan Wallis sobbed, hands covering her face.

"You have to do something for these people," Esmeralda begged. "Give them release from their agony if nothing else."

Wails and moans of anguish rose around the plaza. The damp ground began to give off tendrils of steam from the recent rain. Eli surveyed the carnage and his stomach roiled. Heartsick, he despaired of what he knew should be done. His words were twisted with his pain.

"I . . . *can't*. They've . . . they've a right to live, too."

"You know better," Ed Hendrickson confronted him, his face grim. "For the love of God, I don't like it any better than you. But . . . what else can we do? There's no doctor here, and even so, what could he do? We can only prolong their suffering and torment."

Eli stood for long, silent minutes, head bowed, deeply examining his inner being, his strength and weakness, his moral fibre and the tough calluses of frontier living for more than twenty years. With a stifled groan he turned to the anxious folk gathered around to deliver his heartrending decision.

"Ed, you, Barleycorn and me will attend to those who are hopeless cases," Eli finally responded.

Together they spread out to fulfill their unpleasant and sorrowful task.

"By the balls of Coyote," Red Hair swore lustily. "We were driven out by a force so small we could have crushed them like an egg shell. We learned something, though. Of the two *pen-dik-olye* women, one was the wife of the scar faced One Ball."

"Yes, so it was," Alchise declared. "I saw her clearly."

"We must make plans to capture her and return her to the people," Red Hair stated.

"Why?" Cuchillo, a youthful warrior demanded. "They were mighty fighters, those white-eyes. We were four hands and one when we attacked Sunset Rock. Now we are but two hands and three. Five of those are wounded. He whose true name we must not speak resides with his ancestors. There is no one to claim the woman."

Red Head looked scornfully around at the wounded men, the crude bandages on horses that had been bullet-scraped. From their position high atop a small mesa, they could see the dust trail of those who had surprised them. They went south, toward the bend of the Gila and the way into Mexico.

"Have you the heart of a rabbit?" Red Head snapped. "We are still more than they are. We've got the advantage. Also the woman deserves punishment for betraying her man, the one we speak of as One Ball. We'll let the people decide her fate when we have captured her. Now, here is how we must go about it."

*   *   *

Only half a day's ride separated Eli Holten's caravan from the big bend of the Gila River. Another full day would see them in Mexico. Holten pushed his companions to maintain good speed, though he stopped well before darkness, some three miles North of the bend in the sluggish flow that marked the summertime channel of the Gila.

"We'll make camp here," Eli instructed when the wagon had pulled up and the animals were being staked out on a picket line. "We'll want to prepare in the event those Apache renegades figure out they outnumber us. Barleycorn John, Ed, Luke and Peter, set to gathering up that driftwood. We'll use the smaller pieces for the fire and the big hunks for breastworks. Place those on the rim of this depression, facing outward with the river at our backs. If you ladies will assist Carlos, I'm sure we can enjoy one more good meal before getting into dangerous country."

"If that doin's back at Hobart wasn't dangerous, what do you call it?" Joan Wallis demanded.

Eli offered a faint smile, the tormenting image of little Jimmy's trusting face floating in the forefront of his memory. "That's behind us now. Hopefully it will remain so. In the event it doesn't that's why we're making this into a small fort."

Esmeralda Escobar could clearly read the torment in Eli Holten's eyes and pinched expression. Over the long hours of the afternoon and through their somber evening meal, compassion melted the icy curtain she had erected around her emotions. Putting aside her continued pique at being so summarily transported out of his life, she came to Eli in the lingering twilight and placed a small, soft hand on his shoulder.

59

Eli sat on the riverbank, facing southeast, staring toward the distant rounded nubs of purple mountain tops that were beyond their point of no return, deep in the Sonoran desert. He stirred only slightly at her touch, and did not even look up. They remained that way for long, quiet minutes. At last Esmeralda sighed and broke the reverie.

"It was truly an act of mercy, Eli. I know you're crying inside now, and your grief doesn't show. But we all feel it. Oh, of course the Church condemns such an act, but how inhuman and cruel to let small children and fatally wounded people suffer for even a minute longer, let alone how many hours, before they found peace. It was a fine and courageous thing you did, no matter how you see it. Whether you know it or not," she went on hurriedly, afraid he might speak and break the spell before she had it all out.

"Whether you know it, one of the reasons I love you so is because you are so much the man. *Muy hombre*, as we say it in my language. And you remain more *hombre* than any man I know."

Esmeralda knelt beside him then and encircled his neck with her lovely arms. Her kisses, light as butterfly wings rained on his hair, ears, neck and cheeks. Slowly Eli began to respond. He opened the narrow, painful ball of his recollections and became aware of the heady scent of sage, mesquite and lupin. Bird calls reached his consciousness. It was never a question of arousal. The carnal aspect of their reconciliation never registered. Slowly Eli rose, took Esmeralda by one hand and led her to the tent erected a short distance from the others by her direction.

They entered and disrobed silently. Embracing, skin against skin, they felt a warmth and soul blending that went beyond mere erotic desire. With whispered words of sweetness they cleaved together and became as one. Sorrow and regret found no place to lodge in the love-scented darkness and fled the tent for other roosts. Their amorous coupling washed out pain and renewed hope, love and a bright horizon, beyond which lay a clean, new tomorrow.

CHAPTER 6

With an expression which Eli Holten had come to know meant concern, Ski-Be-Nan-Ted wished them well and remained at the small stone cairn that bore a bronze plaque that identified the border between the United States and Mexico. The caravan departed across the line into Sonora. The Apache sergeant stood by the hammer-head of his lank mount and watched, unmoving, while the riders and wagon dwindled into tiny dots on the red-brown of the desert floor. His thoughts turned to the charge he had been given and he spoke curtly to the men around him.

"We go back Yellow Mud (Gila), make meat. Long wait," he spoke in the gutterals of the Athapascan tongue.

Out ahead of the caravan, refreshed, if not light-hearted, Eli Holten surveyed the countryside and considered the whole grim affair of Hobart in a new light. His heightened sensibilities quickly discerned not a whit of difference between Arizona and Sonora, as to terrain, flora or fauna. More populous than its northern counterpart, Sonora had a comforting scatter of adobe houses, small and low to the ground, that spoke of the thousands who populated this barren waste. Few owned the land they worked, he reflected. Yet their fierce loyalty to the *patrón*, as the Mexican people called the owners of large holdings, and to their country was legendary. Armed with this knowledge, his first experience with it turned out to be disconcerting.

Three small, naked children hid beneath the legs of two adults at the side of the road. At the approach of the wagon and large number of horses, they had whipped off their straw hats and held them across their chests, heads bowed. Upon discovering that the mounted persons were not Hidalgos, let alone Mexican, the adult males' expressions became sullen, lips down-curled, obsidian eyes cold with resentment. The youngsters scurried to hide and peek out big-eyed.

"Pinche gringos," one of the men snarled. The other spat on the road in front of Eli's horse.

"Go back nort' gringo peegs," he grumbled in broken English.

"¡Que vergüenza!" Esmeralda spat from the wagon seat. "Shame on you," she repeated. "Don't you know your betters? I am Doña Esmeralda Escobar y Portales, daughter of Don Francisco Escobar of Rancho Fortunado. *Ustedes deshonoran su patrón."*

Off came the hats again and the expressions changed to hang-dog servility. *"Dispense usted, Doña* Esmeralda. We beg your pardon. We did not know. These men who ride with you, they are gringos, no?"

"Circumstances compel that for the time being they are my *caballeros.* They are to be treated as such, *¿comprende?"*

"Sí, Doña Esmeralda," they chorused.

"Ride on," Esmeralda commanded imperiously.

Didn't take long for her to pick up the habits of her

class, Eli thought with cynically-tinged admiration. Perhaps, though, it would work to get them all through with whole skins.

Holten's hopes were unfounded, he quickly discovered. Distrust met them wherever they went. The deeper into Sonora they traveled, the more people they encountered who greeted them with scorn and contempt. Later into the afternoon, Eli located the tall palms and lower, pale green cottonwoods that signaled an oasis. When they drew nearer, buildings became distinct and Eli figured it to be an inn of sorts.

La Puerta del Sol, the Gate of the Sun, indeed turned out to be an inn. The keeper of the *posada* greeted them effusively under a portico of thatched palm leaves. His expression went blank and unassuring when he recognized the six men to be Yanquis. Eli Holten proposed the question of greatest importance in his rapidly improving Spanish.

"We need rooms for the night, food for ourselves and our livestock, and a good night's sleep. Have you space to take us in?"

A scowling forehead topped a wide, white, oily and insincere smile. His thick, black mustache wagged in false regret. "Oh, I am so sorry, Señor. We are entirely filled tonight."

"No room at the inn, eh?" Eli quipped, noting the absence of any sounds within, or any animals in the corral to one side of the building. "Why don't I believe you, Señor?"

"Oh but it is true. No room. No rooms for gringos, ¿comprende?"

Holten's eyes changed to the gray of arctic ice. "I think I do, Señor *Cabrón*. Good day."

"*Vaya con dios, Señor*," the fat innkeeper in the grease-stained, frilly white shirt responded, words sodden with sarcasm.

"*I* could have put that *pendejo* in his place," Esmeralda grumbled from atop the wagon seat. "Why didn't you tell him whom he chose to spurn?"

"Because this is a land of bandits, Es. Such a group as ours, traveling without military escort would be a prime target for them. No reason to let them know in advance we have something of value aboard."

Esmeralda all but simpered. "You flatter me out of my anger, *corazón*. What do we do now?"

"Move on. Set up camp later. Carlos says there is a bluff overlooking a river some two miles or so away. Sounds like a good place."

"Ummm. I think I remember something of it from our, ah, last journey through this country," Esmeralda responded. "Ay, so long ago."

When the weary party reached the up-thrust shelf of land, Eli gave them no rest. He set the men to work digging firing pits, and dragging deadfall cactus and trees into place for the hasty parapets. Others he designated for use as obstructions on the main avenue of attack. Esmeralda and Joan prepared the evening meal. When darkness fell, the work still went on.

"Aren't you taking too much caution, *corazón*?" Esmeralda asked Eli when she approached him while he paused to wipe dampness from his brow. "We'll only be here for a night."

"If we want to be sure it's only for a night, and not forever, we had better be able to defend this place. General Corrington once told me that the Roman legions built a fort each night along their route of march, complete with palisades. They moved a might slowly that way, but they went on to conquer nearly all the known world of that time."

"Now it's Romans," Esmeralda pouted prettily.

66

"Something more to interfere when I . . . when I want to . . . Would you have me sleep alone and cold tonight, Eli?"

Eli produced a big grin. "I'm sure we can do something to prevent that. Meanwhile, I want to see this camp secure. Ed," he turned aside to direct the work. "In that narrow place. String a line from those two mesquite bushes and suspend a long piece of cactus between them at head height for a man on horseback."

Esmeralda sighed regretfully. "When you are through, I'll have only half a man to keep me company. The sleepy half."

"Don't give up hope so easily, Es,'" Eli told her lightly. "Half a loving is better than no loving at all, isn't it?"

Shortly after the journeyers had been turned away from the *posada*, a slender, nervous young man who worked in the kitchen slipped away from his job and walked a horse off into the desert. Behind him he could still hear the innkeeper grumbling.

"Gringo murderers, who wants them around? So arrogant and pushy. Better they stay in their own country, which they stole from Mexico in the first place."

Jorge Nuñez made sure he had removed himself far enough not to excite curiosity from rapid hoofbeats before he stepped into the saddle. The sun had not yet set and it made it easy for Jorge to fix upon his destination in the low, rounded mountains some fifteen miles from the inn. Once secure in his route of travel and of not being discovered, he set out at a fast canter.

Partway through a narrow, steep canyon, a dark

figure rose out of the blackness under a stunted, wind-whipped pinon. Jorge immediately reined in. Moonlight glinted off a rifle barrel, cradled in the indistinguishable man's arms.

"*¿Quen es?*" the sentinel rasped out.

"Jorge," the young man answered, a quaver in his voice. "Jorge Nuñez."

"Why did you come?"

"I have news of importance for El Gallo de Chaparal."

"What is this news?" the sentry demanded.

Jorge mustered all his flagging courage. "It is for the ears of your *jefe*. It is to him I'll tell what I know."

"*¡Mierda!* Don't get insolent with me, little one. I might shoot off your *cojónes*, and that would spoil all of your fun with the little boys, *¿como no?*"

"Leave my private life out of this, you—you barbarian," Jorge bleated.

The bandit guard spoke through a rumble of caustic laughter. "Ride on, my fine little *puto*. Tell your tale to El Gallo. If it displeases him, he'll skin you alive."

Suppressing a shudder, Jorge complied. In a bowl-like depression near the top of the mountain, Jorge located the stone hovel occupied by Fidel Ocampo, the bandit leader known as El Gallo de Chaparal. He scratched hesitantly at the iron-banded planks of the door, and winced at the sound of a growling voice.

"What the hell do you want at this time of night?"

"It is Jorge Nuñez, Don Fidel. I come with important news for you," Jorge managed to squeak out.

"Come in! Come in! I don't talk through doors," El Gallo demanded.

Jorge entered, blinked at the bright yellow light of a kerosene lamp, his eyes stinging from thick layers of tobacco smoke that wafted through the room. He located El Gallo, sprawled in a large, throne-like chair, carved from a single, massive trunk of an unidentifiable hardwood. On the table beside him, which bore the lamp, sat a clay bottle of tequila and three cups.

"Come, sit down, drink up. You look pale as a ghost," Jorge's frightening host invited.

Jorge crossed the hard-packed dirt floor and took a spindly, three-legged chair. He also accepted a cup of tequilla in a shaking hand. He choked on the first swallow. El Gallo snorted amusement through his big nose and slapped Jorge stingingly on his right thigh.

"So, what has our pretty-boy *enteraro* have to tell us?" the bandit chief rumbled.

"E—El Gallo, there is a caravan of gringos, not a large one, that is passing through this country. They have one wagon, the rest are on horseback. Two women and six men. Two pack horses. They carry something of great value, that I am sure of. The gringo men look mean and have hard faces. One of the women, a *Mejicana* I am sure of it, carries herself like a lady of quality. Perhaps there is a profit there for you, no?"

"Six men, eh?" El Gallo mused. "You think they are *pistoleros?*"

"*Sí*, El Gallo. They have that look, and they all carry many weapons."

"Where are they now?" El Gallo snapped.

"Old Rufio at the posada would not let them stay. They went off to the south. They cannot be much further than the Rio Blanco, north of Altar," Jorge estimated.

"Ay-yi, this is a tempting thing you bring me, *chico*. If it's true . . ."

69

"A thousand pardons, El Gallo, I speak only the truth to you. I'm not a fool. Has my information ever been bad?"

Ocampo considered a moment. "No. Not *bad*, but often over-imaginative I would say. Too many times you see wealth where there is none."

"The wagon is heavily laden," Jorge said hopefully.

El Gallo licked thick, dark lips. "¡*Oye*, Guillermo, Alvado, Paco!" he bellowed, summoning his lieutenants. "Come here!"

When the trio of bandit sub-chiefs slouched into the room and arranged themselves on chairs, except for Guillermo Beltran, who draped an arm over the dome of a beehive fireplace, El Gallo had Jorge repeat his information.

"What do you think, amigos? Does this sound like an over-ripe plum, ready for the plucking?" Piece by piece, El Gallo re-examined each element that Jorge had revealed.

"El Ojo, what do you think?" El Gallo solicited from Beltran.

A white grin of teeth slashed Beltran's dark face. "I like it. They are gringos, no? That alone should be reason enough . . ."

"True. But if they are *pistoleros?*" El Gallo countered, playing the devil's advocate.

"There are only six of them," Paco Mendez reminded.

"I say we do it. We ride down on those gringo *cabrónes* and kill them all, take everything they have, even the women," Alvado Castro urged.

"Ay, *certainly* the women," El Gallo replied gleefully. "*Que bueno*. Then that's what we shall do. Thank you, my little capon. You have done us a good service and I will reward you accordingly. Amigos, tomorrow we ride with the dawn."

Dawn brought gloomy prospects to Eli Holten and his companions. They dismantled their camp under an overcast of thick, heavy-bellied clouds. John Oates and Ed Hendrickson advised against leaving the high promontory where they had spent the night. Eli was anxious to get further along their course to the Escobar ranch.

"Them clouds could open up and send us a gulley-washer that would wipe out that wagon and us, too, most likely," Barleycorn John complained.

"Once we cross the river it won't matter that much," Eli Holten countered.

"Unless it floods," Ed advised. "If storms are anything like they are in Arizona, we'd have to be away from the river and on high ground."

"I'm willing to take the chance. And the sooner we get this done, the sooner we get back to Globe," Eli advised. "About a mile to the west there, see those poles in the water? It looks like a good area for a ford and there's high ground within half a mile south. My bet is those poles are depth markers for someone making regular crossings. We'll head for there and see what develops."

With reluctant groans, the wagonwheels began to turn. Eli had spent most of his time the previous evening securing their defenses he had not found time to scout the road ahead. Finding a way off the escarpment became a time-consuming ordeal. When at last they reached the flood plain of the river, the first fine drops of rain had begun to fall.

"This is gonna turn into a real heller," Barleycorn

71

John predicted gloomily as the caravan strung out toward the distant ford.

Riding in front, Eli Holten and young Peter Taylor reached the wide, shallow river first. The rain had increased in density and force to the point it lashed the water's surface.

"You were right, Mr. Holten," Peter sang out. "See those marks on the poles."

Eli had brought along a large coil of rope from the wagon. He undid the bight end and handed it to Peter. "Go on across and string out this rope. Maybe we'll need it to guide on for the crossing. I'll send Ed over to help you when the rest arrive."

"Yes, sir," Peter eagerly acknowledged.

His long-legged grulla gelding managed the crossing well enough and he made the far end of the rope fast around a sturdy cottonwood trunk. By then the wagon rolled up, along with the rest of the company. John Oates looked frowningly at the sky. Ed Hendrickson studied the ford.

"It's gone up half a notch since I got here," Eli informed him.

"Rain up river. That figures. It'll be here damn soon enough. With luck the flooding won't start until after the storm passes over."

"Tie on to the wagon bed with your saddle ropes and help control it going over," Eli instructed.

The men went about their work and started at once into the froth-flecked waters of the Rio Blanco. Eli would cross last, after undoing the guide line from the deadfall to which he had attached it.

"So far so good," he called out cheerfully as he watched the rest.

"Listen," Ed urged from near the far bank.

Everyone became silent and strained to hear something unusual. Eli recognized it first. The rumble and roar of a floodcrest advancing toward them came muted from the southwest. Suddenly the rain became a deluge.

"Ride for it!" Eli shouted.

Lashing the wagon team, Joan Wallis made straining effort to pull ahead in the already clinging mud of the recently sodden desert soil. Behind them a wall of water could be seen now as well as heard. It rushed along, spreading outward and uprooting trees, cactus and other flora with inexorable persistence.

CHAPTER 7

White streaks split the sky, giving birth to ear-shattering crashes of thunder. Water fell in writhing sheets of gray. Hard, sun-baked ground provided little absorption and the deluge quickly formed eroding rivulets that cut their way to add tons of rainwater and soil to the swollen monster that had moments before been the peaceful Rio Blanco. Horses whinnied in fright and shied from objects real and imagined in the swiftly running flood.

"Keep going! Keep on the move!" Eli Holten shouted above the tumult.

His gaze centered on the wagon, which made slow, desperate going against the pull and suck of the dirty brown current. He motioned to Ed Hendrickson and they closed on the lead pair of the team from opposite banks. Bent low, Eli grabbed the headstall of the right lead and spoke soothingly, while urging more speed. Dimly he heard Esmeralda's scream. He looked around to find her safe, but one of the spare mounts cartwheeled down the river course, spinning on the crest. An apparently sharp-ended length of cottonwood limb protruded from the frantic animal's belly. It had evidently been struck a powerful blow under water. Peter Taylor struck out into the stream after the other packhorse. The rain grew heavier.

"We're only knee deep now. Push it, push hard!" Eli urged them on.

"Heeeelp!" Peter Taylor bawled a shout of alarm when his mount slipped and threw him from the saddle.

Exercising great presence of mind, the youthful gunman kept hold of the reins. His horse bore down stiff-legged and resisted the tugging of the racing waters. The beast's head came around when Peter reached the end of the thin leather reins. Suddenly Carlos O'Banyon appeared beside the floundering boy. His short, muscular arm whipped out and yanked Peter clear of the tumbling water.

"There ye are, Petey-o. Safe and sound. Though damn if the exertion ain't caused me critter to pull up lame," he added as they fought free of the frothy edge of the flood.

"There goes our chance for a quick profit," Fidel Ocampo said disgustedly.

From their vantage point on the bluff, the bandit chief and his men watched the water swiftly rise and the flood crest spread across the plain. The bandits had adjusted ponchos over their persons and firearms and wide-brimmed sombreros shielded their faces. Well acquainted with the vacillating nature of these flash floods, they could do little other than sit their horses and watch. When one, then another of the struggling figures broke free of the suction of the torrent, they felt like cheering.

"A truly magnificent sight, no?" El Ojo Beltran spoke with awe.

"Sí, Guillermo," Ocampo agreed. "But remember, we are here to pluck them of their riches."

"Look, look! The wagon is free," one of the bandits pointed out.

"What do you think, *jefe*? When the waters go down we can catch up to them, no?" El Ojo inquired.

"Yes, I think our little attack is on for today, after all," El Gallo purred, eyes alight with greed.

Survive they might have, Eli Holten thought worriedly. Not without paying heavily for it. One of the pack horses had perished, Pete Taylor's mount, and that of Carlos O'Banyon, had strained legs from fighting the flood. Esmeralda and Joan were exhausted and still a bit unnerved. Reluctantly Eli admitted he felt the strain as much as the other men. At least the rain had stopped falling and they had left the swirling water of the Rio Blanco behind.

"We'll rest a while here, then move on," Eli advised his companions.

Eyes large and face pale, Esmeralda appealed to the scout. "Eli, I thought we would all die when the flood caught us. I ache all over. Can't we spend the night here?"

"I think it's wise if we move on. No telling what sort of animals got washed down here and survived. That flood didn't start around the bend there. It began up in those mountains. There could be cougars, bears, any number of critters, frightened and angry and definitely out of their normal territory."

Esmeralda suppressed a shudder. "I see what you mean. How far can we go, then?"

"With a couple of game horses, I imagine no more than another five miles. That should be enough."

Two men afoot, leading their limping mounts, set the pace. The rain-sodden caravan made a bit over two miles when they came upon five men astride the road. Chuy — Jesus — Rodriguez, Arturo Giran, and three other bandits had been sent forward by a circuitous route to provide a diversion. Meanwhile, El Gallo and his remaining men closed in from the rear. One of the quintet kneed his horse and came forward, his hand raised in greeting.

"*¡Oje, hombres!* That was some storm, no? *Gracias a dios,* we were not in the worst of it as you can see. Oooh, it appears you have had some misfortune. Maybe there is something we can do about it."

"*¡Bandidos!*" Esmeralda hissed loudly from the wagon a moment before Chuy drew his Obregon copy of the Colt Peacemaker.

Close on her word of warning, a sixgun crashed loudly near her side.

Eli Holten had seen the prepatory drop of the bandit's shoulder at the moment Esmeralda gave her warning. He rocked back on his Remington and shoved forward as he released the hammer. The round exploded as the muzzle cleared the pocket and sent two-hundred-fifty grains of lead speeding toward flesh. The slug entered the bandit's belly two inches above the navel and did terrible damage to his intestines.

Chuy grunted at the sledgehammer impact and reeled in the saddle. His Obregon fell from nerveless fingers and his horse whuffled nervously until the dying man fell forward and slid off onto the ground. By then the other bandits had produced weapons. Ed Hendrickson and Peter Taylor matched them in speed, and surpassed them in accuracy. Two of the remaining four took fatal hits before their comrades could discharge a shot. The entire encounter lasted less than forty seconds. Powder smoke still hung heavily around the contestants when gunfire erupted to the rear of the small column.

"There's more of them," Holten shouted unnecessarily. "Get to the ground."

Thundering down on the hastily dismounted defenders, Fidel Ocampo's second-rate bandidos appeared to have all the advantage. Speed was on their side, likewise surprise, and numbers. A hail of lead met them, including stinging, maiming pellets from Joan Wallis's shotgun. El Gallo quickly discovered that the gringos could dish out a lot more than they were receiving. He saw one man, Ed Hendrickson, cry out and momentarily grasp his arm. Elation turned to disgust when the bandit leader observed that the gringo had taken only a shallow scrape.

"Turn the wagon," Eli shouted to Esmeralda. "The rest of you, get behind it." He spun to his right and blasted another of the bandits from the saddle.

At a shouted command, the bandits whirled and rode out of range. They paused on a small, sandy hill. Ocampo cursed the foreigners and railed at his men to finish them off quickly.

"*¡Hijo de la chinga!* We have lost six men, with five more wounded. Mass your attack on the left end of the wagon and sweep right through them."

"*Jefe*, these gringos hit what they shoot at," one of the bandits observed.

"*Sí*," said another. "And all too frequently." A puff of smoke from Ed Hendrickson's Winchester Express preceded a meaty smack which silenced the speaker forever.

"Alas for poor Ramon, they also do it at a range we can't hope to match," El Ojo observed as the man fell to the ground.

Fidel Ocampo decided upon a different tactic. He

rode a short way forward and raised his hands to his mouth. Shouting, he addressed his intended victims. "Geev up, *gringos*. Chu do not have a chance. Thees ees *El Gallo de Chaparal*. All men know me and fear my name. We weel let chu live eef chu geeve up withou' a fight."

A Winchester .40-65 round plunked through the upturned wide brim of his huge sombrero in answer. El Gallo's horse shied and he spurred it in a tight circle, showering dust in the direction of the defenders as he streaked back out of range. At once he belabored his men into another attack.

"Here they come," Carlos O'Banyon remarked.

Shooting and shouting, the bandits closed in. Eli barked a command and the small force pivoted on the tail of the wagon, forming a line of kneeling gunmen across the route of approach. At Eli's order they fired in a ragged volley. Two more of the forty bandits went down. Another volley crashed out.

Three wounded men fell from their mounts. One caught a high heel in a stirrup and shrieked hideously as his galloping mount continued across the rocky, cactus-strewn desert. Two of his companions raced after him. With less than twenty yards separating the opponents, El Gallo called off the charge.

"It is unfair that so few could fight so well," he complained. "Eight men dead, twelve wounded. Load your weapons, *compañeros*, we'll attack again."

Several of the bandits looked at him as though he had lost his mind. They reloaded all the same and touched gigantic rowels to their lathered mounts when El Gallo commanded them. Screaming and yipping, the bandits rode down on the inadequate defenses. At a hundred yards they came under heavy, disciplined fire. At fifty yards El Gallo resigned himself to the obvious.

"Pull back, *hombres,* pull back. They are too strong for us. Another time we will get them when they least expect it.

Eagerly obedient to their leader, the bandits swerved away from the deadly guns of the defenders and galloped over a low swale. As they departed, Barleycorn John observed, *"El Gallo,* eh? Looks to me that he's more capon than rooster."

From a distance of two miles, oblivious to the light rain that still pelted them, Red Head and his renegade Apaches watched the abortive attack of the bandits on the small caravan. At first angry that someone would rob him of the pleasure of eliminating the man who killed Ba-coon and took away his woman, Red Head began to see the humor of the situation as the tiny force of six or seven guns held off the four hands of ten bandits.

"Even with such a large advantage, the Mexicans are not such fierce fighters, eh, Alchise," he declared eventually. "See how they scatter."

"I've heard that their ancestors, the Aztecs, believed that it was the noise that made a man fall down. So they do not aim," Alchise informed his leader.

"That's an interesting idea, old friend. Could it be that other tribes saw it the same way?"

"You're teasing me, Dos-Tan-Nanta. Our ancestors always took away their dead and so saw the wounds," Alchise retorted, offended by the suggestion.

"True enough, brother. But we've heard of others who did not learn to aim the firesticks. Now they tend sheep."

"Phaw! The Navajo and the Hopi. Of what concern are they?"

"Long ago they taught our ancestors humility, Alchise. Never forget that. In battle, it is the man who makes no mistakes who is victorious. But come, let's follow the *pen-dik-olye* and see if another opportunity presents itself."

Secure in his mountain fortress, Fidel Ocampo sat drinking *pulque* and brooding. How could they do such a thing? The question continued to repeat in his head, shaming him. Too many men dead. Too many wounded. All his fault.

No! By all the demons in Hell, it was not his fault. It was the leader of those gringos. He had hidden more men in the wagon, a trap of some sort. That had to be it. His own senses, witnesses to his failure, mocked him. There were no hidden men, no invisible army that drove them off. Six men and a woman. Only six gringos and a gringa fired at his men. While he downed more of the potent, milky intoxicant, a seething rage built in Fidel's breast.

His heart ached with the desire to crush these impudent gringo swine. His honor, his reputation, his future tribute from the small villages depended upon it. Word would get around. He would be shamed and made a thing of ridicule. That he could not permit. The gringos must be brought to account.

"Guillermo, ol' frien' . . . th-those gringos, I will crush them. I swear, ol' Ojo, my frien'. I'll do it. I vow on the grave of my mother and by our most holy Lady of Guadalupe. I . . . will . . . grind them . . . into . . . the dirt!" With each word, Ocampo pounded a fist against the table.

"*De veras.* Of course you will, my friend of all these

years. Who else could hope to do so but you? Next time you will destroy them for all time. But no, have something to eat. These *carnitas* are delicious. Teresa fixed them especially for you. Eat a little, compadre."

"*¡Mierda!* I don' want food. I want a bottle . . . A bottle . . . A bottle of mescal."

It would be another of those nights, El Ojo Beltran resigned himself. "As you wish, *jefe*. First you eat a little, then we will get drunk together."

Sister Gloria Maria watched the fight from half a mile ahead, in tight-lipped trepidation. Any form of violence upset her. Her father had been a matador, one of considerable renown. Even as a child she could never stand to attend the corridas and watch the bloody spectacle. She had entered the convent the day after her eleventh birthday. Over the years since, Sister Gloria had sadly found the cloistered life no gainsay against violence. Even the sanctity of the chapel had been invaded by men in uniform, with their guns and terrible deeds when the French had fought a losing retreat against the forces of Don Benito Juarez. At one point or another both sides had used the church and the convent as fortifications. What a terrible toll it had taken.

Before them had come the *Norteños* with their hateful song . . . "Green grow the lilacs . . ."

"Phaa. Gringos," Sister Gloria muttered through clenched teeth.

Even the smell of gun oil, or the sound of joyous fireworks on Independence Day, each September Sixteenth, made her stomach burn and sour. Still, she watched as the powerful bandit force swept down on the strangers in the caravan. When the valiant defenders drove them off time after time she took heart. At last, with the bandits in retreat, she offered up a small, silent prayer to St. Michael. She also urged the good Padre Dominic to hurry them from this place of danger.

They arrived in Altar a good two hours before the unusual cavalcade of gringos rolled into the square. By then, Sister Gloria and others had spread the tale. The outlanders were stunned by their reception.

CHAPTER 8

Waving and calling out words of welcome, shouting shrilly among themselves, a flock of barefoot children met Eli Holten and the caravan at the northern outskirts of Altar. High, purple mountains loomed behind the town to the south and west. From the plaza came the frantic, sharp notes of trumpets, the scurry of guitars and thrum of bass, as the mariachis made bright music for the occasion. Adults along the main thoroughfare cheered and waved. It all served only to confuse and confound Eli Holten the more. The green, white and red of the Mexican flag snapped crisply from a staff in the plaza. At its base, the mayor, uncomfortable looking in a suit and tri-color sash, replete with several medals, stood waiting their arrival. Holten exchanged puzzled glances with Hendrickson and O'Banyon.

"Who do they think we are?" he asked of Esmeralda.

"I . . . I am not sure, *corazón*. They are shouting 'hero' and 'deliverers,' for whatever that might mean."

"Hey, listen to that," O'Banyon called to the others. "That kid's sayin' we conquered the bandits and have freed them from fear."

85

"That couldn't be," John Oates grunted. "We're lucky to have gotten out of that scrape with whole skins. Besides, how'd they know about it ahead of our gettin' here?"

Reining up in the plaza, the story soon became clear. The mayor stepped forward, along with a middle-aged nun and two clerics. "Welcome, gentlemen and ladies to our humble village of Altar. We greet you as liberators who have lifted the heavy yoke of tribute from our shoulders. Sister Gloria Maria here and Padre Dominic witnessed your heroic fight against the bandits of El Gallo de Chaparal. They brought word of how you defeated them and left many of their number dead on the field of honor. We are proud to greet you as friends and as the heroes you truly are. All things in the village of Altar are yours for the asking. Tonight there is a big fiesta in honor of the victory, and you are our honored guests. You will not have to pay for a single thing while you are among us, amigos. Now come, step down and let us give you the *abraso* of gratitude. Then," he added with a broad wink, "we shall adjourn to the balcony of my office across the plaza and partake of a drink or two in celebration."

Stunned to a blank-faced expression, Eli Holten could only mumble, "Well, I'll be damned."

Candles in festive paper lanterns, and bright, brittle mariachi music banished night in Altar. Being the guest of honor, there would be little sleep anyway for Eli Holten and his entourage. Ed Hendrickson and the other men danced and ate with gusto in the central plaza. Seated at a table, Eli and Esmeralda kept company with the mayor and his wife, and several of the town's important personages.

86

Beer, wine and tequila flowed freely. Foods in wide variety kept coming at intervals. Young boys set off fireworks and sent the little girls away squealing. At ten-thirty the mayor called for silence.

A trio of trumpets blared and loud-voiced men repeated the command. When at last the crowd grew still, the mayor rose to address them. Although staggeringly drunk, he controlled his speech and spoke with an exalted note.

"My friends. My comrades of Altar. Thank you all for coming to help us honor these heroes. These six men and two women, without help for any other save God, vanquished the dread bandit, El Gallo de Chaparal. No more will he come for tribute, for he knows we know of his shame and defeat. No more will he steal away our young women. Freedom has a heady taste. We are just beginning to savor of it. Because of these courageous and powerful friends, perhaps we can now look forward to better lives for a while. To you, Señor Holten, Sr. Hendrickson, Sr. Oates, Sr. O'Banyon, Sr. Taylor and Sr. Walker, our most sincere gratitude. May you enjoy long and fruitful lives. ¡Salut!"

The mariachis went wild. In the ensuing whirlwind of dancing, gales of laughter and gusts of conversation, a young, dark-eyed man approached Eli.

"Señor Holten, I am called Salvador Bernardo Aguilar. I am most familiar with this hostile country. It would be an honor and the least of service I can offer to accompany your retinue to Rancho Fortunado," he concluded with a flourish.

"I, ah, appreciate your offer, Señor Aguilar," Eli responded. "We've come a long ways and are growing close to our objective."

"True enough, Señor. But there are many bandits

and, of course, the Yaqui and Apache Indians. Many of the Yaquis. My family has been friends to the Escobars for years and I consider it a duty."

Esmeralda brightened. "Your father is Don Alejandro?" she inquired.

"He is, indeed, Doña Esmeralda. It would be an honor and a pleasure to escort you home."

Esmeralda propelled herself to Eli's support, though a slight frown creased her brow when she spoke his name. "Señor Holten is my escort, *Primo* Salvador, make certain of that. But . . . I think . . . Eli, can't we make a place for my cousin Salvador in our caravan?" she went on in English.

Eli sighed. "If that's what you want, I'm sure we can." He switched to Spanish. "You would be most welcome to accompany us, Señor Aguilar, as we have need of an expert scout who knows this area."

"Well then," Salvador responded, his *machismo* left intact, "I shall be most pleased to do so."

"Let's dance, Eli," Esmeralda suggested.

"Fine with me," Holten agreed with relief.

After a wild turn of the floor, they returned to the table. On the way, Eli signaled Peter Taylor, who joined them. Eli clapped a hand on the youth's shoulder before offering him a chair.

"Peter, I have to admit that I greatly underrated your ability as a gunhand. You distinguished yourself during the bandit attack, and truthfully, I would feel safe trusting you in any scrape we might encounter from here on."

Peter's face turned a violent pink. "I . . . well, ah, gee-dang, Mr. Holten, I don't deserve . . . really I just did what I had to."

"Sit down, Peter and have a drink with us. You did the job of three men in the river crossing and covered yourself with deserved praise in the fight. From now on, you'll take second place to no man in this outfit."

Speechless, Peter sat and drank, shaking his head in ebullient wonder. Mercifully Eli let him go after a few stammered words.

"Take off, Peter. There's a lot more fiesta to enjoy than setting with the old folks."

"Old folks!" Esmeralda took umbrage.

"Well, at least *I* am. And you, too, if you're too worn out to dance again."

"I'll show you," Esmeralda spluttered, coming to her feet.

Off to one side of the plaza, a young man, wearing the clothes of a *vaquero*, kept careful watch on Eli and his companions. His pale blue eyes contrasted with his shaggy black hair, mustache and the sun-browned skin of his face. Few gave him a second look, knowing him to be a tolerated gringo who worked locally on a ranch off to the southwest. In particular he gave his attention to the tall, curly, yellow-haired man in buckskins. Eli Holten, he'd heard the name.

Who hadn't, he thought with disdain. The whole town considered him some sort of deliverer. Ocampo's bandits would be back in a month, spoiling to take out their humiliation on someone unable to defend themselves. Dumb Mexicans would never learn. Meanwhile, gunfighters of this quality represented a real danger. He pushed himself away from the wall and headed toward a water trough which had been filled with bottled beer and icy water. He'd hang around and find out how long the strangers intended to stay. Wouldn't do to strike up a conversation with them, but old Diego would talk a leg off if provided enough beer and a couple of shots of tequila.

Diego Valverde lived up to his reputation half an hour later. "Oh, *sí*, I hear they are going to stay a few days, Señor Veeli. Tomorrow the mayor is having a special church service for them. You got another beer?"

"For you? Always," Willie Harker answered.

He left Diego in a drunken slumber some forty minutes later. He'd learned all he needed and now fretted to get to his horse and head out. At the livery he redeemed his mount and set out across the desert toward a distant, jagged-toothed range of mountains.

Eli Holten turned restlessly in the bed. Beside him, Esmeralda stirred and raised her head. "What's the matter, *corazón?*"

"Two days of this is wearing a little thin," Eli answered with a sigh.

"Two days of making love?" Esmeralda queried, uncertain.

"Of course not. All this partying, the speeches, bands, people cheering us. We still have to get you to your home."

"Why? There is no hurry," she answered him simply.

Wisely avoiding the open door to another argument, Eli kept to the festivities they had been enjoying. "I can't eat another tamale, or a tortilla stuffed with carnitas, or another bowl of menudo. Tequila makes my mouth dry and my head throb. Chasing it with beer . . . well, you saw the fight Luke Walker got into. The smart thing is to move on before our welcome runs out."

Esmeralda considered it a moment. "Perhaps you are right, *corazón*. In the meantime, the hotel is still

90

quiet, everyone is asleep. Why don't we enjoy what we have?"

Eli would talk to Hendrickson and the others at breakfast, he decided, pushing away his relentlessness to fully enjoy their playfull antics. He had no doubt where their adventure would lead.

Willie Harker grunted as his horse dropped a shoulder on the uneven terrain and jolted him roughly. From his position atop the dun pony, Harker could see the top of the mesa and the distant cluster of buildings. T. Luther Hayden would be highly interested in the news he bore. The gaunt, hard-faced leader had made it clear that he wanted to hear about any Americans entering the area. Six gunhawks and a small caravan ought to really light Hayden up, Willie thought with satisfaction.

"Six of them!" T. Luther Hayden shouted, half-rising from the captain's chair in which he took his ease.

"Yes, sir," Willie assured him. "Six men an' two women. Story is they ran off ol' Ocampo and his bandidos."

"No question they're shootists, then. Odds are they're the law," Hayden speculated aloud. "Len, you an' Dave ride back down to Altar and keep an eye on these strangers. Keep me posted on what they do and if they ask any questions about us."

Hayden had good reason for concern. The hollow-cheeked, icy-eyed man had fled the United States ahead of a large posse. Along with him came seven notorious gunmen and outlaws. Their latest joint venture had been the robbery of a bank which went terribly sour. Once across the border the criminal band felt a modicum of safety. Yet Hayden had no illusions about the willingness of certain lawdogs and bounty men who would flaunt the international barrier and drag them forcibly back into American jurisdiction.

Enough judges existed in enough places who earnestly wanted to put ropes around the necks of Hayden and his companions that a simple matter of kidnapping and violating the territory of another nation would not be a bar to prosecution. Murder, armed robbery and rape were all on the list of crimes committed by Thomas Luther Hayden. Likewise on most of the crew who ran with him. Recently a new charge had been added. A term recently added to the lexicons of the more lurid of journalists, anarchy was the latest infamy alleged to T. Luther and his gang.

There had been that small matter of a bomb set off on behalf of striking railroad workers. The contract had been so lucrative T. Luther could not refuse. He and four of his men rode out of Mexico and blew up a railroad depot in Texas. The blast killed twenty, maimed another thirty and derailed a locomotive and four cars, operated by strikebreakers. Someone had seen and recognized T. Luther Hayden. A ten thousand dollar reward had been offered by the governor of Texas. Now the threat of marshals' badges and high-handed arrest procedures loomed larger than reality.

T. Luther's only strength lay in remaining on his mesa. Over the three years he had been in Mexico, men on the run had banded with his original group and now consisted of thirty capable guns. In the interim, T. Luther's black hair had become shot with salt and pepper and his short stature now sported a small paunch. It hadn't affected his quickness with a sixgun, nor his determination to carve out a small empire for himself in the wastes of Sonora.

"Willie," T. Luther barked. "Catch yourself a meal and some sleep. Then I want you to go over in detail everything you can remember about each of those men."

"Sure, boss," Willie answered with a grin.

"Whether they're lawmen or not, something will have to be done about them," T. Luther declared in an ominous tone.

CHAPTER 9

Sunlight sparkled blindingly off the white gesso overcoat of the adobe block church on the Plaza de Armas in Altar. The bronze bell in the curved arch above the doorway clanged loudly. Birds, set aflutter by the tintinabulations, circled the open square as though confused as to direction. Below, the two wagons and many horses of Eli Holten's caravan had been drawn up in line. Children rushed about, shouting shrilly, while the Heroes of Altar said their final good-byes.

Hand lifted high in benediction, Padre Dominic inscribed the sign of the cross in the air over the Americans. "May the Peace and Love of our Lord, Jesus Christ abide with you always. May the power of His angels watch over you and bring you a safe and successful journey," the priest intoned in Latin, then switched to Spanish. *"Vaya con Dios, amigos."*

Early morning of the fourth day since their arrival in Altar brought the males of the expedition a bumper crop of hangovers. Barleycorn John Oates and Eli Holten were the only exceptions. Despite his throbbing head, Peter Taylor wore a broad, silly grin. *Josefina . . . Josefina . . .* The name lilted in his head over and over.

Weren't any boys of fifteen he knew of who did

anything but talk about *it*. Here he'd actually done it five times in the past three nights. Ah, sweet little Josefina, his reflections ran back over time.

She'd been waiting for him that first night. Josefina's smile and sparkling eyes, even in the dimness of the short alleyway, had made him glow warmly, radiating outward from a tightness in his belly. Her hand had been soft and warm when he took it in his callused paw. Afraid she might break, he had barely applied pressure. In his years along the border, Peter had acquired a working knowledge of Spanish, though they spoke with signs and gestures at times when the conversation grew esoteric.

"I am called Josefina. Josefina Gonsalves."

"I am called Peter Taylor."

"Pe-et'r? *Pedro. ¿Es correcto? ¿Pedro?*"

"Yes. That's right, I guess," he had responded shyly.

"Come with me, Pedro, we will have lots of fun."

Peter couldn't keep his eyes off the small, firm mounds of her breasts. While they walked through the alley to another meandering street of dwellings, he learned of her family and that no one was at home in the Gonsalves house. They entered through a low doorway, the lintel of which was a thick, hand-hewn slab, resting atop two uprights of similar rough-finished wood. Josefina had taken Peter's hand again and led him through the darkness to the rear of the house.

"This is the room of my little brother, Ramon," she explained as they passed a doorway. "Here is where my sisters and I sleep."

Had the light been on, Peter would have seen her blush. She tugged impatiently at his hand and he resisted a second. "Come, we go in here, no?" Josefina urged.

96

"Uh—I, uh . . . Sure, I suppose. A—are you gonna put on any light?"

"Just a little one," Josefina assured him.

Suddenly she was facing him, her small, hard breasts pressing against his chest, arms around his neck. Awkwardly, Peter embraced her. Straining forward, Josefina placed her lips against his. They were warm, soft and very alive. Peter had scant experience at kissing girls, even less at what followed.

"Whateryoudoing!" he blurted suddenly through the kiss when Josefina ran her hands up under his shirt and began tugging it upward to his shoulders and neck.

"Undressing you, of course. We can't make love with our clothes on," Josefina answered simply.

"M-m-make love?" Peter stammered.

"First we take off your shirt, then take off mine," Josefina explained as though to a small child. "Then we light a candle and look. After that we get rid of the rest and make fabulous love together."

"We'll be movin' out in ten minutes."

"Hunn-whaaa?" Eli Holten's rough baratone dragged Peter out of his delightful reverie.

"Ten minutes," the scout repeated. "Are you certain you don't have someone to say good-bye to?" A grin spread on the sun-browned, weather-wrinkled face.

"Unnn . . . er-ah, I've a-already taken care of that," Peter babbled.

"Then you'd best be tendin' to the animals, instead of cookin' up a stiff pecker with daydreams," Eli jokingly told him.

"I—er-ah, my God, does it show so clear?" Peter gasped.

"To anyone who's been there before," Eli answered in a gentler tone. "So you found yourself a girlfriend, eh? I hope she made you happy, 'cause it'll be a long way between beds for you when we pull out."

"I—ah, oh, she made me happy all right," Peter responded dreamily.

"Hey, Len, you ever see a sorrier lookin' lot?" Dave Denton asked his partner.

Leonard Bueler gazed after the departing caravan and shook his head. "I've never had enough cash money in my pocket to hang on a drunk like that. If it hadn't been for free, I bet them fellers would never be feelin' so drug out this morning."

"You've got the right of it, Len. So, what do we know of them?"

"Wahl, they not a one mentioned anything about bein' lawmen. They drank more like soldiers than badge toters."

"None of the locals called one of 'em 'Chief' or 'Captain.' Might not mean anything if they're movin' on the sly. You want to keep trackin' 'em and I'll report back to the boss?"

"Now, Dave, all you want is to get back to li'll Anitiacita, eh? Need a little lovin' to put the shine back in your eye, huh?"

"Len, you've got a dirty mind," Dave grumbled.

"I've got a stiff pecker, just like you. Them fellers got all the available stuff an' some that wasn't so available. You wanna put a bet on how many babies is gonna be born here 'zactly nine months from now?"

"No bet, Len. See that pretty little thing sayin' good-bye to the youngest of that lot? I hear he got into her pants right regular, every night of the fiesta."

"The shape she got on her gives me the hanker. We know where that bunch is headed. The Escobar Rancho. Only one way to get there. What say we both report back an' maybe we can hit 'em before they get too far away."

"Good idea, Len. We'll do it that way."

Still eying the passionate and willing Josefina, Dave and Len ambled to the corral for their horses.

With the sun low and orange-red in the west, the wagon and riders cast long shadows to their left. Still a good two hours to darkness, Eli Holten decided to push on a bit further before making camp. Sonny, the scout's well-trained war horse, first noted something threatening. He stopped abruptly, snorted and stomped a hoof.

"What is it, boy?" Eli asked soothingly, patting the Morgan's arched neck. "You smell Indians?"

Sonny shook his head as though to dispute the surmise. A bullet cracked past close to Eli's head, followed by the moaning zipper sound of incoming arrows. It provided the scout a clear answer.

"Damn!" Eli swore. "It's Apaches. Get to the ground, circle the horses on one side of the wagon to form a barricade."

More arrows and hot lead sought them as the cavalcade hurried to comply. Joan's shotgun, in Esmeralda's hands, boomed first. The shot column tore up what appeared to be a clump of sand close by the off side of the wagon. The clump sprouted arms and legs and rose, screaming in agony, to reveal a long-haired Apache warrior. Long familiar with this subterfuge, Esmeralda quickly spotted more of the concealed fighters. The shotgun went off again, another brave howled in pain and then Eli Holten understood and began firing with his Winchester.

Now the humps of sand died with only slight writhing of appendages. Their life's blood drained into the thirsty desert from gaping exit wounds in their chests and abdomens. From beyond a slight rise hoof beats drummed in growing volume. First the large, black-haired heads of mounted Apaches appeared. Then their shiny torsos, painted blood red by the declining sun. Moccasined heels drubbed horses' ribs and the attacking warriors came to a gallop.

"Here they come!" Carlos O'Banyon called out. "Hell bent for breakfast, they are. Jesus, Mary and Joseph, could I ever do with a hundred of those Injun-hating Mezkins right now."

They came to him like grazing deer, these *pen-dik-olye* with the wagon and many horses. Soon his friend of so many years would be avenged. Dos-Tan-Nanta gloated over the ease with which he and his men had established this ambush. Better still, the blind way the white-eyes moved into it. The big one in the lead, with the blond hair, he had seen around San Carlos. He had been with those traitors, Ski-Be-Nan-Ted, Chil-Chu-A-Na, Togo-De-Chuz and others. That strong, black horse he rides, Red Head decided, would make a good mount.

He tensed when the subject of his thoughts stopped and snorted. The short column had reached a point well inside the ambush. The horse, obviously a war pony, had caught scent of the hidden warriors, Red Head surmised. No time to wait longer. With a fragment of mirror, he made a signal for the attack to begin.

A Winchester and three trade rifles cracked from hiding. A flight of arrows whistled off toward the enemy. Instantly the white-eyes formed a defensive circle. Warriors, buried for hours in the sand, rose up at their very feet. It should be over swiftly, Red Head estimated. Then his surprise element began to die swiftly, cut down by the accurate fire of the scout and one of the women. With a wave of his arm, Red Head brought his remaining men to their feet and atop their horses. Uttering a shrill, ululating cry, he led the charge.

Hardly had they crossed a low ridge when Red Head heard a bullet crack by. A spent round he dismissed. Then the pony ridden by his cousin, Sky, folded its forelegs and went down, a slug in its head. Within a few yards steady, carefully aimed fire slashed into his charging warriors. Two more horses went down, screaming like hurt children. A man died, his neck broken when his mount collapsed under him. At fifty yards a bullet grazed Red Head's left shoulder.

The wound burned and stung, but bled little. Red Head urged his men on. It did little good. The volume of fire increased and forced those in the lead to swerve away from the stalled wagon and its ring of defenders. Angered and frustrated, Red Head assembled his band again and harranged them into a second attack.

"We've got 'em on the run!" Luke Walker exclaimed.

"Don't stop now. Pick off the stragglers," Eli Holten commanded.

"Will they come back?" Esmeralda inquired tightly. She surrendered the shotgun to Joan, who reloaded and set it to one side.

"I don't know. From what I've seen so far, Apaches never do the expected," Eli stated. "Pass around a canteen and some of those cold tamales. We need to keep up our strength."

"Oh, God, look!" Joan Wallis cried. "They're coming back."

"Everyone hold your fire," Holten commanded. "Wait until they're in to fifty yards, then take careful aim and fire in volley. Shoot the horses. The men will be easier to hit on foot."

"We cannot lose many more horses," Alchise advised. "If we do, we will not be able to get away before the Mexicans send soldiers."

"We came to take back the woman of my friend who is no longer with us," Red Head growled. "Are we coyotes to slink away with our tails between our legs?"

Alchise sighed. "If this attack fails? If we lose more horses? Then what, my friend?"

Red Head shrugged. "When that happens, if it does, then we'll worry about it. Now we must attack again. Being still in this heat, without water or relief will soon tire them. Then we can make easy work of it."

"FIRE!" Eli Holten shouted above the tumult of galloping horses and Apaches discharging rifles.

Three warriors were swept from their mounts. Two horses died. Red Head and Alchise looked on in disbelief as the whites rallied and continued to direct accurate fire into the ranks of the attackers. Stung by the insult of defeat, yet unwilling to risk more men,

Red Head called off his band and they rode swiftly out of sight.

"That's it for now," Eli remarked. "We managed to hold off two charges. We've plenty of ammunition in the wagon."

"Problem is, how do we take it with us?" Carlos O'Banyon queried. "Two of the mules are dead and half the horses. We're as good as on foot."

Checking quickly, Eli verified this gloomy report. They could use surviving horses to pull the wagon, the mules would do for pack animals, yet that literally left all but himself and Ed Hendrickson afoot. They would, the scout grimly acknowledged, be easy targets if the Apaches decided to attack again.

CHAPTER 10

Horses and mules will not pull together. That fact was known to everyone on the caravan. While Peter Taylor set about selecting the mounts best suited to substitute for the mules, everyone cleaned their firearms and reloaded. Eli examined his companions to assess the damage. Barleycorn Oates had taken an arrow through the loose skin under his left armpit. Eli cleansed it and wrapped Oates' shoulder in a bandage.

"You'll heal," he assured the young gunhand. "Ride in the wagon for a day or so. Now go get something to eat and rest until we're ready to start out."

"We're going on today?" Oates asked.

"Right. We don't want to stay here with the dead animals, right? Also every mile we cover puts us that much closer to help if the Apaches attack again. And don't forget those bandits. That fellow El Gallo might like to take another crack at us."

"Ummm. We're not in very good shape if either of those things happens," Oates observed.

"True. So far we've been lucky. If we hold out a little longer we'll be through the mountain pass and . . ."

"And close to San Patricio de las Palmas,"

Salvadore Aguilar put in as he came to where the men sat in the shade of the wagon. "It's getting late."

"True," Eli responded. "We'll make a mile or so and camp."

"One of the water barrels was hit with a bullet," Aguilar offered.

"I saw it. We'll have to make do with what we've got," Eli answered. "At least until it can be patched and refilled. It looks like you, Ed Hendrickson and I are the only ones with horses to ride. I'll scout ahead and locate a campsite. You and Ed keep watch on the flanks and rear."

"Mighty big job for two men, Eli," Ed Hendrickson remarked as he joined the group.

"After I locate a spot to camp, I'll ride back and help cover," the scout told him. "What worries me more than right now is tomorrow. We'll be starting into the foothills and even more vulnerable."

Relentlessly the yellow-white furnace high in the sky sucked moisture from their tired bodies. Water dwindled rapidly as men and animals consumed more to replenish what they sweated away. Through the long morning the caravan had been on a gradual, though taxing upgrade that led through ever increasing mounds, mesas and broken hills. Ahead, the only pass beckoned from the lush, cool promise of distant mountains. Shortly before eleven o'clock, Eli Holten called another of their frequent rest stops. Immediately Salvador Aguilar produced a thick poncho from his saddle bags and wormed his way into it.

"We must all put on more clothes to keep in the cool and save moisture. The sun will suck water from your skin if it is exposed."

"I never heard of puttin' on clothes to keep cool," Peter Taylor remarked in a surly tone produced by heat exhaustion and strain.

"Think about the Indians," Aguilar suggested. "They put on layers of blankets to keep cool and travel for hours without water, while we take off more and more clothing and slowly die of thirst."

"Huh! I never considered that. I always thought they were just too dumb to know how to keep comfortable," Peter replied. "I got a rain slicker I guess I could use."

"No," Aguilar cautioned. "That would only steam cook you. What you wear has to be able to breathe, but slowly."

Peter untied his bedroll and wrapped a blanket around his shoulders. "Be darned, the sun don't seem to burn as much," he blurted in surprise.

"Time to get rolling," Holten advised. "Pass a canteen, one swallow each. Petey did all the stock get watered?"

"Small pailfull each, Mr. Holten," the youth answered.

"Then we'll set out for that patch of shade ahead. Those cottonwoods will shelter us during the midday break. Salvador, you take the point."

From a cleft in the rocks a small, silvery spring nourished the cottonwood trees. Incredibly cold, the travelers found it a haven from their past ordeal. Amid expressions of relief, and restocking of water, Esmeralda and Joan set about preparing a meal.

"We'll wait here until the sun breaks over, around four or so, and move on until dark," Eli informed them. "Enjoy your hot food now. There will be no fires at night."

"Eli," Esmeralda started, then hushed at his sudden frown.

"A fire in this sort of country would be a beacon to those Apaches, or any other wandering Indians, not to mention our friend Ocampo and his bandits. No light of any sort."

Everyone took turns lying in the icy seep from the spring, wetting clothing and parched flesh. The meal was tasty, the last of the fresh food from Altar. With ice cold spring water and coffee to wash it down, the outing took on an almost picnic atmosphere. By four o'clock, the entire party felt refreshed and ready to move on. Despite this beneficial reprieve, Eli Holten could not shake a powerful premonition that they somehow started off into worse danger than they had encountered so far.

From the brow of a large sand hill, T. Luther Hayden and his gang observed the desperate situation of the suspected lawmen. The would-be empire builders had come upon Eli Holten's caravan at midmorning. Outriders spotted the slowly trudging column and reported back. From then on the gang shadowed their progress. During the noontime halt T. Luther called a council of war with his lieutenants, Jake Jackson and Dave Denton.

"That wagon's carrying a hell of a load," Denton opened.

"Could be nuffin' but a cookstove," Jake Jackson suggested. He wrinkled his mahogany brow and mopped at the accumulated perspiration with a checkered bandanna.

"Or it could be a chest of gold coin to pay for help to capture us, Jake," T. Luther offered. "Whatever, they've not lost a man as yet. From the looks of those dead animals, they ran afoul of Indians. That they fought off the Apaches or the damned Yaquis says something. Here's what we'll do. I'll take the main

108

force forward, toward the pass. Dave, you stay back and follow them. Jake, take ten men and go off on their south flank. Keep out of sight but in contact so you know when to sweep in on them."

Jake spread his hands, pink palms upward. "Boss, you know how hard it is to not be seen in this country. How we gon' do that?"

T. Luther studied Jake Jackson for a long moment. "You'll think of something, Jake. I'm sure of that. There's not another one of your people who have adapted to the desert like you. When was it you deserted from the Army?"

Jake scratched his mop of wooly black hair. "That was back durin' Reconstruction. In Texas it was. Been so long I like to forget."

"Killed a white officer, didn't you?" T. Luther pressed.

Anger glittered in Jake's obsidian eyes. "No call to bring that up," the huge, thick-shouldered black man growled. "He done wronged me and the other colored troops. He called us 'nigger.' Worse even than the Rebs. Said he didn't fight to free no slaves. He was after a chunk of that rich Southern land. Said we'd be stoopin' our backs in *his* cotton fields like always, onest the gov'ment got some sense again."

"Never you mind, Jake," T. Luther soothed. "Down here you're gonna be a regular king. You're my strong right arm and I couldn't do without you."

"Why, thank you, Tom Luther. I reckon if I have one man keepin' an eye on those folks from time to time, we can be in position right when you wants us."

"Get to it, then, both of you. They'll be pulling out before long and I want to have a good head start."

"*¡Mierda!*" Fidel Ocampo exploded as he hurled

the stub of a smelly cigar to the hard desert floor. "Dead animals, Apache arrows, but no graves. Where are the men? Are they all still alive? I want answers, *burro*," he growled at the leader of the trio sent out scouting. Miguel Chavasos, weighted down with crossed bandoliers of .45-70 cartridges, merely shrugged.

"Where did they go, Miguel? Surely you must know that," Ocampo prompted.

"To the Southeast, of course, *jefe*. To Dorado Pass."

"They're far ahead of us. We must make haste. Get going, *bufón*, go find those gringos."

One small, bowl-like valley lay between the caravan and the higher mountains. Dorado Pass, over a mile high in the sawtooth escarpments of the Sierra Madre Occidental, revealed itself by a jagged line of pale, blue-white sky. Eli Holten decided the far side of the dish would be suitable for camp. That way they could start the climb fresh in the morning. Taking the lead, he set the wagon and the foot-weary men in motion.

A dozen yards short of the center of the bowl, an arrow appeared as though from nowhere and buried its tip in Eli's left side. The projectile entered from the front and sent waves of pain radiating outward from the ragged channel of its passage through flesh. Reflexively, the scout drew his Remington and fired in the direction from which the shaft had come. Then he looked down at the fletchings that rose and fell with each breath. He knew that the jagged stone tip would be protruding from the skin in back. Biting back the agony, he dismounted.

"Apaches!" Salvador Aguilar shouted, bending to

draw his rifle.

"Not again," Joan Wallis cried with a note of desperation.

The tall, brown grass came alive with wriggling bodies. Choosing their targets carefully, the Apaches moved in closer before unleashing their full firepower. This tactic allowed their intended victims time to prepare. Barleycorn Oates and Ed Hendrickson sheltered behind the wagon, rifles ready. Young Peter Taylor climbed to the wagon box, saw to setting the brake and securing the reins, while Esmeralda hefted his sixgun and Joan nervously fingered her shotgun. Holten and Aguilar threw their mounts and sheltered behind them.

"Cooo-weee-kweee!" Red Head signaled and rose with his warriors for the attack.

Hidden among the rocks, T. Luther Hayden and his gang watched the cavalcade ride down into the shallow valley. They had arrived only a short while before, guided by their scouts. As a result they had missed the earlier deployment of the Apaches. So carefully had Red Head concealed his warriors that when they attacked Hayden was taken by surprise every bit as much as the hapless people of Eli's column.

"What the hell? Where'd those Injuns come from?" Hezakiah Thorne blurted out.

"Keep it down," Hayden hissed. "Even with all the shooting, one of those Apaches might hear."

"Apaches? This far south?" Len Bueler queried.

"They don't look like Chinamen, do they?" Jake Jackson growled.

"What do we do now, Boss?" Willie Harker asked.

"Wait a while, I suppose," Hayden answered

111

uncertainly. "If we rode in there, those damned Apache snakes would turn on us, you can be sure. For the same reason, we can't stay around to see how it comes out."

"Look there," Dave Denton whispered urgently. "One of them just went down. From the looks of it, the Apaches are gonna finish them off for us."

Hayden scowled. "I've got no love for the bloody-handed redskins, but if they can bring an end to the threat of these strangers, I'm all for it. Save us the risk of being exposed, too."

"Well then, what do we do?" Jake Jackson asked.

After a moment's thought, Hayden announced new plans. "We'll pull back through these rocks, get the hell away from here. After the Apaches finish their dirty work, we can come back and check on these strangers."

"What if it turns out they ain't lawdogs?" one of the gang inquired.

Hayden shook his head. The idea hadn't occured to him. "Then for a while I'll feel like some kind of son of a bitch for not drivin' the Injuns off. But that, too, will go away. Now keep low and don't let the Apaches see or hear you."

Driven by renewed desire for revenge, the Apaches swarmed over the beleagered defenders. Fighting closed to a few feet, then face-to-face. A vicious struggle set up between Ed Hendrickson and three of the hard-faced warriors. Barleycorn John Oates butt-stroked a screaming brave and turned to help.

Fire followed the solid impact of an Apache lance, which its owner drove into Oates' side. The stone tip spread ribs and slid deeply into lung tissue, then pricked his heart. Oates quivered like a beached fish and let go of his empty rifle. He only faintly heard the report of Eli Holten's Remington from close at hand.

Eli's bullet put a hole where the Apache's nose had been and bulged his eyes. Blood gushed from the mouth of Barleycorn John's killer as the hot lead destroyed his brain. Joan Wallis blasted another warrior into eternity with a load of buckshot. Dust rose from the trampled ground, mingling with powder smoke. A bullet slapped heavily into the side of the wagon near Eli's head and he ducked, involuntarily crying out at the pain in his side. Peter Taylor appeared on his left, a knife in one hand, still bloody from slashing open an Apache's belly.

With care Peter grasped the arrow through Eli's side and cut away the shaft near the fletchings. Then he shoved the remainder out through the exit wound. Eli bit his lip and gasped only once during the crude operation.

"You did that rather well, Petey," he managed to say.

"I may be a kid, Mr. Holten, but I've fought Apaches before on my folks' place. No time for a bandage, will you be all right?"

"I'll manage. Take care of yourself. And get a gun."

"Ran mine dry, no time to reload. That 'Pache over there's got a Winchester. If you can shoot him, I'll get it."

"I've never been so wrong about someone in my life," Eli said wonderingly as he took aim at the indicated warrior.

Two hundred fifty grains of lead blew away the side of the Apache's head and Peter Taylor snatched his rifle before it hit the ground. He turned part way to give Eli a friendly wave, then gut-shot a warrior charging him with a lance. Incredibly, more Apaches

113

joined the wild melee around the wagon. Then, unexpected and unexplained, shouts of alarm came from the outer fringe of milling warriors.

Gunshots exploded beyond the scene of battle. Three Apaches fell kicking in the dust. More weapons opened up and a wild, keening cry filled the air.

"Yiiiiiiii!"

Hoofbeats thundered and a swarm of some thirty Mexican riders swept across the bowl toward the battle. They wore large charro hats and fired wildly as they closed on the fleeing Apaches. Most of them continued on, in pursuit of the Indians, while four men skidded their horses to haunch-squatting halts beside the wagons. Eli Holten blinked his eyes and brushed away rivulets of muddy sweat. At first he couldn't believe it. Then the short, stocky man on the big dun horse spoke and removed all doubt.

"*Hola, gringos.* Chu are lucky we like keeling Apaches more than robbing *gringos,* no?" Fidel Ocampo saluted them, grinning. "Today we have — how chu say? — a truce. My men weel hunt them down while you make it safely to the foot of the pass. We enjoy the sport of running down these long-haired dogs."

"We're, ah, much obliged," Eli mustered his surprise enough to say.

Ocampo produced a scowl. "We weel do chu no harm thees time. But remember, you owe something to El Gallo de Chaparal. And *mañana tambien es una otra dia, ¿verdad?*"

Eli had no doubt as to the implied threat. "Yes. Tomorrow is certainly another day."

CHAPTER 11

Smoke from the cookfire rose in lazy spirals above the ring of rocks which surrounded it. An owl hooted pensively and mosquitos buzzed about, while crickets and frogs set up competing choral groups. Eli Holten had taken advantage of their unexpected respite to press further into the pass, their night camp a good thousand feet above the highland mesa country where they had encountered the Apaches. Wondering what tribute Fidel Ocampo would exact, and when, he sat alone under a spindly, resin-rich pine and smoked a cigar. Her chores completed, Esmeralda found him there.

"*Corazón*, you find too many things to worry about," she declared as she settled gracefully beside him, an arm draped on his shoulder.

"For good reason. We've lost one man already. I'm just considering what we might encounter ahead of us," Eli replied absently.

Esmeralda produced a little pout, ruby lips glistening in the moonlight. "It is less than fifty leagues to Rancho Fortunado. What can possibly happen?"

"In under half that distance we've twice been attacked by Apaches and once by bandits. According to your cousin, Salvador, the other side of this range is Yacqui country. Do you believe they'll be any less hostile?"

Esmeralda put two slim fingers to his lips. "Don't be so angry at what you cannot control, *corazón*. Tonight there is a beautiful moon, we're off the desert and safe for once. I would think your mind would turn to other things."

"Such as?" the scout asked, certain from his own quickening of breath that he knew the answer.

"Before long we will be where I must appear completely a lady. No hint of anything, ah, irregular must be allowed to show. Surely you would not refuse to help me store up happiness now while we can against those bleak days to come?"

Eli cupped one of her firm breasts. "If you're asking if we'll make love tonight, you're wasting words." Esmeralda stiffened beneath his touch. "No," he said gently, "you've taken the wrong meaning again. After what we've been through, I have every intention of ravishing you until your eyes cross." Their lips met. A soft moan escaped Esmeralda and she began removing her clothing.

"Yes," she hissed when she sensed his resistance. "Right here, under this tree, under the stars. Now, beloved. Take away the fear and stink of death. Make me whole again."

Instantly aroused by his own need to deny the horrors of the day, Eli joined in the disrobing and marveled at the alabaster sheen of her flesh, dappled by the shadow of pine needles in the moonlight. Forgoing words, he silently and eagerly positioned her against a cushion of their clothing and with a swift, determined stroke entered with such great force that it elicited a cry of surprise from deep in her throat. Esmeralda sucked in air and fought to dispell the delicious dizziness created by his fullness within her.

Then urgently, as though prolonging life itself depended upon it, Eli began to surge in and out. Abandoned to their primal urges they coupled with animal ferocity. In a whirlwind of delirium the tensions and terrors whisked away, leaving peace and a growing contentment. Idly, before her last tether to reality sundered, Esmeralda wondered what others were doing that night.

Fidel Ocampo hurled a stone into a shale slide and cursed as the clatter died after the rocks stopped shifting. "No Apaches and no loot from the gringos. Guillermo, did I make a fool of myself?"

El Ojo pulled a long face. "No, compadre. An act of gallantry may seem foolish, but each one is a measure of a man's greatness in the eyes of heaven."

"You are philosophical tonight, Ojo. The gringos have many things of value. I can smell it. Yet, we'd be eternally shamed to let those savages murder them. Tomorrow is another day. I told the gringo leader that. Perhaps the time will come when we can reward ourselves for our good deed, no?"

"If you say so, Gallito."

They walked their horses along an indistinct path on the far side of the mountains, in a high plateau area rich in grass and water. Where could the strangers be going? Up here were only the ranchos of the Alvarado and Escobar families, some starveling villages of their *campasinos* and a couple of churches. Fidel Ocampo reviewed this in light of what they had seen of the gringo caravan. With the suddeness of a lightning bolt he saw clearly.

There had been a woman, a *young* woman. A *Meji-cana*. She would be about the age of the Escobar

117

girl who disappeared some six or seven years ago. Could it be? If so, the gringos' wealth would be a living, breathing one, a treasure that could be held for ransom. Great visions soared in his head.

"Guillermo, tell the men we will camp here for the night. Tomorrow we will take another look at these gringos."

"I found out who them Mezkins was who interfered with the Apaches yest'day," Jake Jackson informed T. Luther Hayden shortly before sunrise.

Hayden squatted by a small fire, pouring a cup of coffee from a large blue granite pot. They had heard the flury of shots that ended the attack on the suspected lawmen and sent a man back to check. He had reported a large force of Mexicans, possibly *rurales*, driving off the Indians. Frustrated in obtaining an easy solution to their problem, T. Luther had led his men off in a safe direction and settled in for the night. Now he rose expectantly, gesturing to the coffee pot.

"Pour some and tell me about it, Jake," he told the black man.

"Sho' 'nuff." Jackson squatted and filled a tin cup. "Those were Fidel Ocampo's men. Nothin' but plain ol' bandits."

"Not so plain, Jake," T. Luther corrected. "Ocampo takes tribute from half a dozen villages, he's robbed a couple of gold shipments from Durango and even taken on the Federales one time. We're not large enough to attract his interest or to do anything about him now. But the time will come when we will have to work something out."

"You mean join up wif him?" Jackson asked, incredulous.

118

"Neither he nor his men would go along with that. You know Grover and Jim have gone to talk with those Texas boys. If they throw in with us, it'll nearly double our number . . . and, they have a Gatling gun."

"That Grover Hanks is a smooth talker," Jackson observed. "He could charm the birds down outta the trees. We git that big, Ocampo's bound to come lookin' for us."

"Right you are. Only we'll find him first. The folks in Altar threw a three day party for those strangers and all they did was run off Ocampo sort of temporary. What do you think they'd do for the men who broke Ocampo's power entirely?"

A gleam of avarice bloomed in Jake Jackson's eyes.

Eli Holten called a halt when the wagon crested the top of the pass. They looked down on a broad, spreading plain of tall, undulating grass, with here and there a few cactus and paloverde trees to remind the optimistic that this was still arid country. The sun beat down warmly in the thin air and Holten estimated they would be down on the plateau before it set. Surely they could make the rest of their journey without incident, he ardently hoped. They had better, he corrected, because the ammunition had dwindled to what each man carried.

The caravan had passed through the mountain village of San Patricio de las Palmas in early morning. There had been no ammunition to purchase at any price. News of marauding Apaches had reached the small community ahead of them and an air of worried expectation diminished hospitality. Salvador Aguilar estimated another thirty leagues to travel, some sixty miles. They had purchased burros

119

in San Patricio. The stocky animals now hauled most of the expedition's supplies and baggage. It allowed everyone to ride, though not with the greatest of comfort. Eli surveyed his small command and raised his Stetson to wipe away perspiration.

"I hope everyone's done enough gawking. We've got a ways to cover yet," he announced. "Salvador tells me there's little chance of the Yaquis raiding around here. They've been pushed farther north and west. All the same, everyone keep a sharp eye."

Eli's admonition served them well. They traveled through the day and the next without incident. A lingering sunset of spectacular colors, seen only in these mountainous regions, lighted their way into the first of several villages on their route. The weary travelers took rooms at the inn and luxuriated in baths, fresh food and comfortable beds for the first time since leaving Altar. Ed Hendrickson had a bit too much to drink and Joan Wallis quickly took him to task.

"Ed, you promised to stay off the booze after that despicable display in Altar," she complained with a fishwife sharpness.

"I only had a couple of tequilas," Ed responded defensively.

"A couple of *bottles?*" Joan snapped.

"That ain't fair!" Ed roared.

"I hate a drunk!" Joan shrieked. Her palm made a sharp popping sound when she slapped his face.

Ed grabbed her, and for a moment it appeared he would smash a balled fist into her face. Then he took on a smug expression and spoke softly. "It's a long walk home."

"I ain't going, except with the man who brung me," Joan riposted.

Ed chuckled throatily and nuzzled his lips in the

hollow of her throat. Taking her hand, he led her from the common room of the posada toward the cubical they shared. Business returned to normal. Some twenty minutes later a knowing chuckle spread among the *vaqueros* and Eli's crew when a high, giggly voice came from down the hall.

"Ooooh, Eddie!" Then, a few moments later, "Ummmm, you're not so drunk after all."

Two Knife peered long and hard at the strangers. What were they doing in this country? He had been a small boy the last time his people had fought with the Long Breech Cloths. Now they came boldly into what had once been Yaqui country. It had to be them, the long, shaggy hair, tied off with calico cloth or strips of rabbit skin, high-topped moccasins, the long panels of their breech cloths, which gave them their name, nearly touching the ground. And they hunted the pale-skinned ones who had passed before.

It would be nice to kill some of the pale-skinned people. He would be a hero among those of his village when he returned, Two Knife thought. But it would not be wise to cross the Long Breech Cloths to do so. He, Puma and three others had come hunting deer, a prized addition to their usual fare. A successful hunt would also bring them honor, though not like the scalps of the pale ones. Yet their old enemy stood in the way. A hand pressed gently on Two Knife's shoulder.

"I hear your thoughts, young one. I, too, would like to sink my war club into the skull of one of the Long Breech Cloths. We are too few and they too many. Perhaps another time."

Two Knife looked at old Proud Lizard. "Perhaps my sons, when I have them?" he asked with the bitterness of the teenaged boy he was. "Or my son's sons will strike at them?"

"Watch them, my grandson, and learn. For only a fool says he cannot learn from his enemy."

It far from satisfied Two Knife. He gusted out an impatient sigh and continued his surveillance of the stalking Apaches. Moving like snakes through the tall grass, the long-haired warriors slithered toward where the pale-skins made camp for the night. The youth caught at his breath when he thought one of the unsuspecting victims saw an Apache. When no alarm followed, the boy shifted position himself to keep the main force of Long Breech Cloths in sight. He shivered with excitement when he observed the silent signal that called for an attack.

"Not again, gawdamnit!" T. Luther Hayden grumbled mostly to himself. "It's those damned Injuns."

From a screen of trees Hayden and his gang watched the Apache attack develop. Confident that they would be able to strike down the strangers without interuption, the outlaw band had arranged themselves in wait for the caravan. It had no sooner shown itself over a low swale when Hayden detected movement in the tall grass.

"How'n hell did they get here?" Dave Denton asked in a whisper. "They was scattered all to hell an' gone by the Mezkins."

"You oughtta know Apaches well enough to not be surprised, Dave," Hayden returned. "You lived in Arizona long enough."

"Too long by my lights. What do we do now?"

"Bide our time," T. Luther suggested.

* * *

Eli Holten reacted instantly to the first shots fired by the Apache ambushers. Bullets and arrows went high and wide of the mark while he rallied the others.

"They're on foot and we're mounted. We'll make a run for it."

"They have to have horses close by," Ed Hendrickson advised.

"I know it, but it'll take time for them to get to them. Es, get that wagon rolling. The rest of you cover them. I've got one thing to do first."

While the wagon team labored into a gallop, Eli dismounted and produced two lucifer matches. These he struck to light on an outcrop of rock. His right hand fisted his Remington and he sent careful shots at the hidden enemy while he ignited the dry, brown grass. Flame licked up eagerly, propagated and spread rapidly. Eli swung into the saddle and raced after the caravan. Howls of outrage came from the Apache warriors.

Running ahead of the flames the Apaches set out for their horses. Red Head cursed in Spanish and quickly outdistanced his followers. In less than two minutes they lashed their mounts into a neck-stretching run. Red Head's keen eye gauged the distance separating him from the fleeing quary and decided they would catch up within a mile. The horses could not sustain their speed for much longer than that.

Ahead of the Apaches by half a mile, Eli Holten closed on the wagon and urged more speed. Riding on the right side Salvador Aguilar wore a cheerful grin. He maintained it as they thundered over the uneven ground, following the crude tracing of a trail. More riders appeared in front of them. It appeared to Eli that the Apaches had sprung an effective trap. Still Salvador kept on grinning. The distant riders loped towards them.

Distance closing, Eli recognized the firearms in their hands. While he watched, the men wearing wide-brimmed sombreros — Damn! It must be Ocampo's men — raised their weapons and fired. Eli nearly returned a shot when a shout from Aguilar stopped him.

"No! Don't shoot. They've come to help."

Bullets cracked over their heads, moving in the direction of the rapidly closing Apaches. Another ragged volley erupted and the riders spurred their mounts. Salvador waved enthusiastically.

"They're *vaqueros* from Rancho Fortunado. Escobar's men," he gleefully told Eli. "We are blessed with great good fortune."

"Let's stop and turn back on the Apaches," Eli suggested.

"Wait until they ride through us, Señor Eli," Salvador advised. "Then our combined fire will surely drive off *los indios.*"

Smirking a bit himself now, Eli complied. The *vaqueros* shouted greetings as they streamed through the harried riders, who slowed and turned about. In moments the heavy volume of fire ripped apart the Apache line and the survivors scattered wildly.

"We've done it! We've done it!" Peter Taylor shouted wildly.

"At least now I can be sure there'll be no more interference," Eli sighed gratefully.

CHAPTER 12

Red Head raced toward a stand of trees. Bullets cracked through the air around him and his men as they strove to escape the unexpected arrival of the vaqueros. When they neared the stand of willows they saw more forms waiting among the drooping limbs and narrow trunks.

"There are more of them," he shouted and swerved away.

Thundering toward a low ridge they came upon more of the Mexicans, who opened fire and drew back. Red Head signaled his men and they dashed off in a wild disarray, retracing the ground they had previously covered to the only source of escape. With the Escobar *vaqueros* in pursuit, they disappeared over the swale, leaving the field empty, save for a few riders who stopped by the caravan.

"There are more men over there, *jefe*," one of Ocampo's bandits reported. "The Apaches tried to break out through the trees and turned away before they came our way."

"Go and see who they are, Paco," El Gallo ordered. "Be careful and do not be seen."

"Who could they be?" El Ojo inquired.

"I do not know, amigo. We will pull back before the *segundo* and his *vaqueros* become curious, no? When Paco returns we'll know more.

Half an hour later, with considerable distance between the scene of the abortive attack and the retreating bandits, Paco rejoined them to make his report.

"They are gringos, *jefe*. You know the ones, those on the Mesa de la Plancha."

El Gallo developed a far-away, speculative look. "Ay, *sí*. I know of these *ladrónes*. Bandidos like ourselves. I have thought to squash them like bugs. I wonder what their interest in these gringos happens to be? Perhaps we should find out? We will return to the mountains and I'll send men to negotiate with these gringo bandidos."

"Are we goin' all the way back to Flatiron Mesa, Boss?" Hezakiah Thorne asked when the band of Americans slowed to a walk.

"No. We'll pull back in the mountains a ways and work out some plan to deal with those strangers. There's a wide spot in the road this side of the top of the pass, San Patricio de las Palmas. We'll hole up there until we think of something," Hayden decided as they rode.

"Won't the locals object?" Jake Jackson asked.

"Not after we get through with them," T. Luther assured him. "They'll be tame as puppy dogs."

"How d'ya think El Gallo will react to our takin' one of his towns?" Dave Denton queried.

"I think El Gallo will be too busy dodging Apaches to be bothered by that," T. Luther said with smug confidence.

*　　　*　　　*

"Por dios, I still don't believe it. Doña Esmeralda? Little Esmeralda who was lost to the *indios?"* Roberto Pastore, *segundo* of Rancho Fortunado exclaimed wonderingly when Esmeralda Escobar stepped lightly from the wagon.

Eli had summoned her when the *segundo* and five of his men halted to check on their condition. Gray laced his hair now and at first Esmeralda didn't recognize the under-foreman of the ranch. When she heard him speak her eyes twinkled with recollection and genuine affection.

"¡Tio Roberto!" she cried joyfully. "It is you. I'm back, *Tio mio.* All of me. This—this is Eli Holten, a scout for the *Norteño* army. He rescued me from the Apaches and brought me home. H-how is Poppa?"

Pastore smiled broadly, a wide white slash in his walnut-hued face. The sun and weather wrinkles seemed to come alive with happiness. "In good health, prosperous and strong as ever, *gracias a dios.* And you, Señor," he addressed to Eli. "You will be received as a hero, that much I assure you. My men are too wise to chase the Apaches into the mountains. They will return in a little bit. While we wait, we can sit in the shade, sip some wine and talk of old times, no?"

"We, ah, don't have any wine along, Señor Pastore," Eli answered plainly.

Pastore beamed again. "Ah-ha! We were working cattle close to here and came with all speed when we heard the first shots. That didn't keep me from having a couple of bottles of good Alvarado *vino* in my saddlebags to refresh the men at our noon meal, *como no?"*

A vague memory of gunfire from another unexpected quarter teased at Eli's consciousness. It prodded him to ask, "Hadn't we better move a distance away from here, Señor Pastore?"

"Why? We are in no danger here. And call me Roberto. I'm only the *segundo*, not the *mayoral* or the *patrón*."

"You're my precious Tio Roberto," Esmeralda injected, giving him a big hug. "You used to let me ride on your horse with you before Poppa would get me one of my own."

Somewhat off balance at this show of affection, Roberto Pastore whipped off his huge charro sombrero and fanned himself. "Ah, those are tales of days long gone by. We'll enjoy them together cara mia, over there at our leisure. Miguel, bring the wine, *por favor*."

Tough, wiry young men, two of Roberto's *vaqueros*, galloped ahead to bring the remarkable news of Esmeralda's deliverance to the main ranch house before the slow-moving party arrived. Women stood along the way through the village established right outside the hacienda, waving their aprons, while children ran and shrieked and goggled at the gringos. Several of the headquarters attendants mounted their horses and raced back and forth, discharging sixguns. In the doorway of the church, Padre Tomas repeatedly blessed the newcomers as they rode by. The tall, thick double doors in the high wall around the hacienda swung inward and the wrought iron gates flew open.

Each section was propelled by a small, barefoot boy in white cotton pants and shirt, cut in the square-yoke style ancient when Cortez first arrived. Framed in the arched portal stood Don Francisco Escobar y Portales and his doughty housekeeper, the gray-haired Señora Anna Maria Del Prado. Tears ran down her seamed face and she jigged up and down in excitement. The little cavalcade drew up in front of the hacienda and introductions were made.

"Señor," Don Francisco addressed to Eli. "You are the man of the hour, day and year to us at Rancho Fortunado. Today you bring home to us our little girl, thought lost forever to the heathen savage Apaches. I am moved to weep with joy and relief, as you can see this old crone beside me is already doing."

Anna Maria del Prado acted scandalized. Don Francisco winked at her and put an arm familiarly around her shoulder. Then he continued. "There is no greater pleasure than for a man to welcome his daughter. Unless it is to welcome her rescuer. *Mí casa es su casa*, Señor Holten. Anything that the estancia of Rancho Fortunado can provide is but yours to ask. Now come, leave your horses to the *custodio de corral*. Urraca will find you rooms. You may refresh yourselves and then join us. It's nearing the hour of sixteen o'clock and time for a light almuerzo."

"Thank you, sir, we're beholding to you for that," Eli answered simply.

"You, my princess," Don Francisco addressed to Esmeralda, "will have your old room. Everything is . . . is as you left it."

Eli bent close to her ear and whispered, "And you thought you'd not be welcome?"

"*Sí, jefe*, the gringos have taken over San Patricio," Jose Garza told Fidel Ocampo. "They shot the *alguacil* and his two policemen, and the mayor and took over the town. They are drinking and making sport with the *mujeres*. They don't even have a watch out. Everyone is getting *borracho*."

Anger clouded Fidel Ocampo's normally dark face

black. For a long, silent moment he seethed with rage over this insult. "San Patricio is my town, our town! These gringos overstep themselves."

"There are many of them, *jefe*," Garza paused and looked around the clearing in the mountains where the bandits had camped. "Nearly as many as we are. And, like the gringos with the wagon, they are good with their guns."

That gave Ocampo reason for thought. If these men from Flatiron Mesa had confidence enough to openly defy his power, even in a fringe place like San Patricio de las Palmas, they must be strong indeed. Maybe it would be wise to play them along, find out more before acting . . . perhaps rashly. Forcibly he calmed himself.

"The time has come, I think," Ocampo said to the men listening intently to the conversation, "for us to make some sort of proposal to these gringos. After all, they're in the same business, no? Lupe, Jose, you will go with El Ojo to sound out the gringos. Offer them our friendship. Find out what it is that brings them here. It obviously has something to do with the gringos with the wagon. If so, tell them we might make common cause over it. Hurry. I want you to report back before sundown tomorrow."

Savory smoke rose from the huge fire pit behind the main, two-story, Escobar hacienda. Situated beside the kitchen and storehouse building, its demands kept busy two slender youths barely in their teens. They carried billets of wood to the flaming pile, which would be rendered down to a bed of coals suitable for cooking. A sleek, three year old steer had been butchered the previous afternoon and hung up to be drawn. It would be affixed to a long spit, with four pointed tines at each end, and slow cooked over the flickering bed until pronounced just right. Revolving around its own axis, it would be basted by its own juices and generous brushings with a mixture of beer, melted lard and lemon juice. Two hogs had been slaughtered to provide carnitas and four goats would later be roasted in clay ovens.

The festive menu didn't end there. Huge bowls of *masa* were being converted into tamales, using trims from the butchered animals. An antique pot of *menudo* simmered on a tiled stove. Tortillas by the hundreds would be called for. Two wooden horse troughs had been filled with beer and ice. Mariachis tuned their instruments and gave off short riffs of songs they wanted to rehearse. A fiesta, although not on so grand a scale as at Altar, had gone into preparation.

That would come later, the large, explosive burst of jubilation, when all the villages of the rancho would be invited to join in celebrating the return of the beloved daughter. There would be fireworks and Japanese lanterns, feasting and drinking, dancing and singing, a *charriada* for the *vaqueros* to test their skills, even a solemn High Mass of thanksgiving. Don Francisco sat at his desk, meticulously planning the events for this forthcoming extravaganza.

He had spent most of the morning after the joyful return working on it. That had left the affairs of his daughter up to others in the household. Naturally Esmeralda gravitated to Eli Holten. She found him on the parapet of the outer wall, staring pensively at the mountains they had come through, purple on the distant horizon.

"What are you thinking of, *corazón?*" she inquired.

Eli started slightly and turned to her. "Ah-ah!

131

Careful of that. You're the one who cautioned against any show of familiarity."

Esmeralda flushed slightly. "No one can hear us here, they can't even see us. I'm glad you remembered. Now, tell me, what is it that bothers you?"

"All these people who were after us," Eli began uncertainly. "The Apaches, El Gallo's bandits . . . somehow I get the feeling they won't have given up so easily. And there's, ah, some other factor . . . something I'm missing, that involves folks we haven't even seen as yet."

Light laughter from Esmeralda tingled the air. "Unseen enemies? Oh, Eli, you're imagining things."

Below, on the hard-packed dirt of the square in front of the hacienda a small boy set off a string of firecrackers. Eli's face went blank as images began to play back in his mind. He wet his lips and snapped thumb and finger together.

"Yesterday, when the Apaches attacked again. There were more people shooting at them than the *vaqueros* and us. It happened after they broke and started to find a way to escape. Red Head's band tried both flanks, remember? Both times they turned away and took the more risky route of running back toward the mountains. There was firing from our left, from among the rocks. But I get the distinct impression that the Indians encountered someone else in those willows."

"Some of Tio Roberto's *vaqueros*," Esmeralda suggested.

"That could account for those who did the shooting. But the others, who held their fire and withdrew? I . . . don't know."

Tinkling laughter came again and Esmeralda linked her arm around Eli's left elbow. "We're safe

132

here. No one would dare attack us. Come on, take me down to the stable. I want to show you a favorite place of mine when I was a little girl. The stream I told you about."

"What about your *dueña?*"

"Oh, her," Esmeralda said coquettishly. "I've quite worn her out and she's taken to her room to recover. We'll have the whole afternoon entirely to ourselves."

"At the place where your urges first awakened," the scout completed. "I have a feeling that if I don't live to regret this, I'm going to enjoy it a whole lot."

One colossal hangover drove a spike into the head of Jacob Jackson. Red-eyed, cotton-mouthed, he gagged over the smell of his own breath as he forced himself upright. The knock came at the door of the low hut off the plaza in San Patricio and rebounded in his skull like a bass drum.

"I'm comin', damn you," he growled.

He slapped the Mexican girl beside him on her bare rump. His unwilling companion of last night, she came upright with a fearful squeak, grabbed her clothes and clutched them to her as she scurried to the far side of the room.

"*Vayaté,*" Jackson growled as she began to dress. He swung long, black legs out of the bed and drew on trousers. Unsteadily he made his way to the door. "What is it?"

Len Bueler stood there, his buck teeth shining in the harsh sunlight. "There's some Mezkins here to see the boss. He wants you an' Jim Simmons to come over for the palaver. He's at the posada. They've got coffee."

"Thank God for that," Jackson groaned. "I'll be

right along. Go find Jim."

"We have come," the medium-sized bandit, who looked to be in his mid-thirties, explained when the American outlaws assembled, "as representatives of Fidel Ocampo, El Gallo de Chaparal, the bandido leader of Sonora. He bid us bring you these presents to prove his good will. For you," he said to T. Luther Hayden, "who is the leader, no? He gives this, a fine, hand-worked silver bit and bridle set. It once belonged to a *Coronel* of Federales, who made the mistake of trying to chastise El Gallo."

T. Luther accepted it gravely. It was a beautiful piece, he had to admit that. Expensive, but it would look nice on his line-back dun. "Your *patrón* is most generous," T. Luther said expansively. "I shall prize this always."

"To your *Tenientes*, he charged us to present these." Guillermo Beltran snapped his fingers and the bandits beside him produced two leather-covered cedar boxes, which they opened, to reveal matched pairs of Obregon copy Colt Peacemakers. One set was chased in silver, the other in gold.

Jake Jackson's hangover dissolved away as he examined the lavish firearms. El Ojo made note of that and smiled a secret smile. El Gallo had surmised that if the lieutenants received the more valuable gifts, perhaps one of them could be turned against the leader. Guillermo had never seen a man so dark before. Not just brown, but actually black, with a purple sheen. The pink of his tongue and the inner linings of his lips made sharp contrast when his avarice betrayed itself by a savoring lick.

"These belonged to a *haciendado* who refused to extend hospitality to El Gallo. He will have no further need of them where he is now. So, with the compliments of El Gallo de Chaparal, I give these things to you. I hope that they're not found to be insignificant.''

"Not 'tall," Jackson mumbled, reaching for the gold engraved revolvers.

"To the contrary," T. Luther effervesced. "They are generous to a fault. We're grateful for your leader's esteem. What else brings El Gallo's representatives here to see us?''

El Ojo looked T. Luther hard in the eye. "San Patricio de las Palmas is one of several villages under the protection of El Gallo. Your presence here, and the manner you have treated the villagers, is an insult to El Gallo. However, your daring and achievements are impressive. Enough so the El Gallo seeks to open discussion regarding a possible alliance.''

T. Luther pulled a long face. "Go on.''

"You are aware, of course, of the gringo strangers with the wagon?" Beltran queried.

"You mean the Yanqui lawmen who've been battling the Apaches?''

"*Sí*, if that is indeed what they are. El Gallo finds their presence in Sonora to be undesirable.''

"So do we. For a number of reasons, I might add," T. Luther advised him.

"They are now taking shelter at the *estancia* of Don Francisco Escobar y Portoles, Rancho Fortunado. Don Francisco is a wealthy man. He has a strong room filled with silver ingots and bags of gold coin, there being no trustworthy bank near at hand. For too long a time Don Francisco has been holding out against El Gallo's attempts to liberate this vast fortune. Now he harbors these undesirables. If it is your wish, as much as it is El Gallo's, to remove these minor irritants, perhaps we have grounds for mutual assistance and profit?''

135

T. Luther Hayden considered it for a long moment. El Gallo might be a buffoon and a wind bag, but this one was a consummate politician. Nearly as good as himself, T. Luther acknowledged, at arranging things. It could be they had common grounds. On the other hand, an attack from within would be easier than one from outside. Fortunately Jim Simmons had just rejoined the gang.

He brought along good news. Twenty assorted wanted men from Texas and Indian territory were on their way, led by Grover Hanks, who brought with him the Gatling gun. Perhaps it was time to deal with El Gallo. An attack from within could be worked from two ways. T. Luther produced a broad smile.

"Gentlemen, let's sit down and discuss it," he boomed with false sincerity.

CHAPTER 13

Following the first spontaneous fiesta, Don Francisco planned a series of visits, each with its own fabulous party, to reintroduce his darling daughter to hidalgo society in southern Sonora. Far from the forbidding and unforgiving atmosphere she envisioned, her father's effusiveness, more than any of the others, was genuine in his joy over her return. A niggling worry remained that she might be rejected, particularly by the women of their social class. It compelled Esmeralda to attempt a frank revelation of her experiences over the missing seven years.

". . . so Miguel tried to give us the mercy of a swift death. He managed to serve Doña Alicia with a saving bullet, but the Apaches killed him before he could shoot me. When the Apaches got the coach stopped, they pulled me out and ripped off my clothes. They began to touch me . . . everywhere," Esmeralda lowered her eyes and blushed at this point.

"*¡Por dios,* I don't want to hear it!" Don Francisco exploded. "I don't need to know of your tribulations whilst among the savages. *Gracias a dios,* you are home safe and unharmed."

Spreading through her, the warmth of gratitude and relief eased Esmeralda's conscience. She put on a faint smile and addressed the matter of the social calls. "Poppa, must we make all these visits?"

"Of course. I want to show everyone that you are my beloved daughter, every bit as much as before the, ah, the accident."

Demurely lowering her eyes again, Esmeralda gave voice to her inner fears. "Thank you, Poppa. I—I couldn't stand it if you . . . if you . . ."

Moving swiftly, despite his age, Don Francisco hurried around the desk in his study and embraced his daughter's shoulders. "Now, now, nothing will ever be said about it. Go and find Doña Matilda and your friend who rescued you. Make something of this day together and tomorrow we will leave for the Alvarado rancho."

"Yes, Poppa," Esmeralda meekly said.

After her departure, Señora Anna Maria del Prado entered. She bustled about in an obvious huff, then turned to Don Francisco, fists on hips, the faint mustache on her upper lip fluttered with the vehemence of her words.

"And what of her life with the Indians? They certainly despoiled her. Of course I am delighted and grateful to God that she's back with us, and such matters don't offend me. But your attitude hides an ugly truth. She's damaged goods now and will never make a desirable match."

Don Francisco raised a placating hand. "There's no shame in what she had to do."

Affronted, Doña Anna spluttered her words. "*You* can say that? You, who are a man and set the standards by which a woman like Esmeralda is considered ruined and degraded? You're letting your father's love blind you to the truth."

"*¡Tontería!*" Don Francisco all but shouted. "After all, isn't there a little *indio* in all of us? That

138

proves, at least to me, that there had to be someone doing a little mixing in the past. I will hear no more of it. Do you understand me?"

Hands pressed together, Doña Anna made an elaborate, mocking curtsey. *"Sí, patrón,"* she drawled in elaborate sarcasm.

Eli Holten chaffed at the delay in returning to Globe. Don Francisco had announced at the big fiesta that he would suitably reward the brave men who had brought home his daughter. So far that largess had not been bestowed. Eli had a strong suspicion that this promise, like everything else, was subject to the *mañana* philosophy of life in Mexico. The elderly *haciendado* would surely keep his promise, but life with him moved in terms of seasons and years, not hours and days. Not that Eli minded keeping company with Esmeralda.

Here on the rancho there was no talk of marriage. It eased the strain he had felt behind his eyes since the lovely young woman had first broached the subject. They had only the one occasion to be alone and intimate, what with all the celebrating and visits by neighbors and local relatives. Some of these, he noted with relief, were young and given to casting amorous glances Esmeralda's way. Now he rode beside Esmeralda, with Doña Matilda, her duena, hard-faced and hawk-eyed, a few paces behind.

They were on the way to the village of Villa Merced. Eli had welcomed the suggestion. Peter Taylor had gone there late the previous afternoon and had not as yet returned. Curiosity aroused, Eli intended to locate the spirited youngster and bring him back to the hacienda. There were, after all, some unfriendly types around.

"There's a little open air eating place in Villa Merced," Esmeralda rattled on. "I used to love going there as a little girl. They served the most delicious *cabritó*. You like roasted goat, don't you, Eli? Anyway, I thought we would stop there. And I want to see Señora Espinóza, who used to make my dresses. I need some new ones, if I'm to become a society item. All these parties. Poppa makes such a fuss over them."

Eli listened with only part of his mind. His major concern remained with Peter Taylor.

Peter Taylor lay on the narrow bed and looked up at the thatch roof, seen through the gaps in the occotillo vegas. He floated in a delightful lassitude, his youthful energies drained and a warm glow of pride in his achievement shielding his body from the still cool air of the small adobe room. Beside him, the slender, bronze-skinned girl stirred slightly and draped an arm over his bare chest.

Renewed shivers of delight coursed through Peter's body. At the big fiesta, the girl, Sylvia Bargas, had made clear a definite interest in Peter that went beyond dancing and dining together. He learned of where she lived and came to Villa Merced to pay a call. They talked and strolled and she flirted outrageously by local standards. Later in the evening she joined him in the room he had rented and they made marvelous love through the night.

"Señor Tay-lor, Señor Tay-lor," the skullery boy at the posada called through the barred door early the next morning. Your *patrón* is here. The Señor Holten."

"Oh, God! Oh, damn! I—I, ah, I—er, ho-ho-hold on just a-a-a-a-aaaaaah!"

140

Sylvia had slipped out of the room and safely away through the back door by the time Eli Holten knocked for admission. Peter still had to button the fly of his trousers. Shirtless and in bare feet he hurried to open up before Eli smashed the thin portal down.

"What's the matter? Has something happened?" he blurted to stave off the words that would accompany Eli's thunderous expression.

"I should ask you the same question. You said nothing about staying here over night, Peter. Could you explain yourself?"

Peter tried to frame an answer while the scout's well-honed sense of smell picked up the aroma of passion that gave him the whole explanation. He fought to suppress the grin forming on his full lips. His eyes held a knowing twinkle. Inexperience blinded Peter to this and he stammered out the first thing that came to mind.

"I, er-ah, well, I got drunk. Yeah, I drank too much with some fellows in the cantina and decided to stay over."

"In the process of getting drunk, I gather you also got laid," Holten returned coldly. He tried to remain stern, but his sense of humor and his knowledge of himself got in the way. "Given the circumstances, by God, I would have, too," Eli gasped out through a chain of hiccoughing guffaws.

"Señores y Señoras," Don Francisco bellowed loudly to his many guests. "It is my distinct pleasure to welcome you to my home. This time we celebrate the gallantry of those brave men who safely brought my daughter back to me."

Tears filled old Don Francisco's eyes as he gazed fondly at Esmeralda and saw in her the clear, beloved

141

lines of her mother's face. Had she not looked so much like his long-departed wife, he had to admit, he might not be so forgiving of her apparent cooperation with her captors. Don Francisco sighed audibly. He could not generate any wrath or feeling of disgust toward this lovely, sweet-tempered child.

"Es difícil vivir de acuerdo con las normas que tradición establecen," Don Francisco murmured aloud.

"¿Que?" Eli Holten inquired politely from his side.

Startled that someone had heard him, Don Francisco blurted out, "I said that it is hard to live up to the standards tradition has set for us."

"Quite true," Eli answered levelly.

Don Francisco's announcement that this fiesta was in their honor had taken Eli off guard. At last, perhaps, they would receive the promised reward. Further still, it should insure their safe passage back to the border. He looked over the smiling faces and the plethora of food, and shed a bit of his cynicism.

A huge fiesta, grander than the first, swirled around him. Goats and pigs had been roasted, gallons of menudo produced, along with rice, beans, guacamole and thousands of tortillas, with all the condiments. Horse troughs, filled with beer and chilled by icy spring water, lined the square. Tables groaned under the weight of food, bottles of tequila, pulque and brandy. Don Francisco finished his announcement and produced from an iron-strapped chest beside him leather bags heavy with gold coins.

"Now, before the revelry gets under way, let me reward you all for your part in this miracle. These bags contain but a small portion of the Escobar fortune. Even so, I think you will find them most satisfactory, for each contains gold pesos in the

142

equivilent of three thousand American dollars. Spend them in good health."

Astonished at the old Don's generosity, Eli could only stammer his thanks. "On b-behalf of my comp-companions, I thank you, Don Francisco. I-It's all together too generous a reward. We did little beyond escorting the wagon."

"Not so, my fine, modest friend. I heard in detail of your heroism. Esmeralda took great pains in describing your feats of courage. Believe me, you have earned every bit of this modest approbrium. Now, let us drink and eat and give ourselves to enjoyment."

Seething with anger, Fidel Ocampo lay on the far side of a low sandy hill. He observed the activities at the hacienda through a pair of field glasses taken from an imprudent captain of *rurales* who had dared to attack El Gallo's band with his paltry fifteen policemen. To Fidel these were a symbol of his power as El Gallo de Chaparal. When he had attended the personal conference with the gringo bandit, T. Luther Hayden, El Gallo had expected at least joint command. By rights, he believed, he should have commanded the main force.

Instead, he and five others had been given the demeaning task of being forward scouts, to spy out the activities of their would-be victims. *¡Mierda!* Fidel had boys of eighteen who could do that. Yet, there he lay. Through the moderate enlargement of the twin lenses he watched the opulent celebration get under way. He counted nearly eighty people present. More important, most were women. The grandees were having a fiesta. All the better. Their minds would not be on standing off an attack.

"Pablo, ride to . . ." Ocampo's face twisted in

143

disgust, "where the others are and tell the gringo *jefe* that it looks like there will be a fiesta here for at least three days. Many wealthy landowners are here. We'll have good pickings."

"And you, *jefe*? What will there be for you to do?" Pablo asked with the innocence of youth.

"I will wait," Ocampo spat out the words like a bad taste in his mouth, "and watch."

"The plan will be ready soon, *jefe*," Pablo insisted optimistically. "Then you will lead us in a great victory."

Ocampo grimaced. "If God is willing, I shall." *Or rather, if the gringo Hayden is willing,* his thoughts tormented him. "Leave at once. And keep low so the patrols of *vaqueros* don't spot you."

Silently, Pablo obeyed.

T. Luther Hayden looked up from the crudely drawn map and produced a satisfied smile. The intense light in his eyes made his slight stature insignificant. The brace of Merwin and Hulbert revolvers, worn in cleverly designed shoulder holsters made the menace in his expression more meaningful. He brushed at a shock of frizzy brown hair and stabbed a long, aesthetics index finger at the diagram of the Escobar hacienda.

"This will make an excellent headquarters for our little empire, Jake," he told the huge negro at his side. "I want it taken with a minimum of damage."

"There'll be a lot of bullet scars in the outer walls," Jake Jackson suggested.

"They can be patched. I don't want any burning. See that everyone understands that. Especially those stupid bandits Ocampo brought us. Also, arrange for a good wagon, with a tight cover, to transport the

144

Gatling gun. We don't want knowledge of it reaching our enemy."

"Can do, boss," Jackson assured him. A wide, white smile illuminated his ebony face. "There gonna be lots of gals there?"

"Plenty," Hayden granted. "Enough even for your prodigious appetite. Only, try to keep your pecker in your pants until we've subdued the entire potential fighting force. This diagram Ocampo drew is excellent. I only wish his map was as detailed. Look here. See the places men can hide and fire down on an attacker?"

"Seems tough, all right. How we gonna neu— neuter—ah . . ."

"Neutralize?" Hayden offered.

"Yeah. How we gonna neutralize those strong points once we get inside?"

"Shouldn't be any problem, if everything goes according to my plan. You see, I figure to force a surrender with the Gatling gun. That, or kill almost all of the defenders before we breach the wall."

CHAPTER 14

Music filled the air at Rancho Fortunado. Outside the sharp, syncopated stanzas of the mariachis set feet to tapping even on those who were not dancing. Inside, strings and a pianoforte provided waltzes and mazurkas for the more refined guests. Eli Holten held Esmeralda in an approved fashion as they made their way around the floor. Her skirts swirled widely as her small, slippered feet described the intricate pattern of the dance.

"I feel like I'm floating," she enthused brightly.

"It's the wine," Eli suggested.

"No, it's being close to you, after so long. I want . . . I want you so badly. I *need* you deep inside me, to make me feel real and alive again. Those visits Poppa took me on. I died of boredom."

"What? With all those handsome, aspiring young men panting after you?" Eli teased.

"Callow youths," Esmeralda sniffed. "No three of them half the man you are."

"In quality . . . or quantity?" Eli continued to torment.

"*Both!*" Esmeralda replied with vehemence. "Oh, how I want to slip away from all this, while everyone is occupied, and make ferocious love."

"How can we with that *dueña* of yours giving us

147

the hawk eye?''

A mischievious gleam came to Esmeralda's eyes. "There is . . . I think . . . one way. Let's get Matilda drunk. Then we can . . .''

"She has a hollow leg," Eli interrupted.

"She has no tolerance for tequila," Esmeralda giggled. "If I mix some with the wine punch . . . *¡Ay de mí!* All your chatter-chatter has made me break stride. I look clumsy as a cow. Let's stop and plan this further.''

Eli steered Esmeralda to a dimly lighted alcove and they sat in a hand-carved wooden loveseat. Esmeralda fanned herself with a scrap of lace kerchief. Her breasts heaved in a tantalizing manner that occupied the scout's full attention for several moments. Esmeralda's dueña hovered close-by, barely out of earshot.

"It'll be easy," Esmeralda suggested. "She dearly loves her wine punch. All I need do is slip some tequila in a cup, pour for her and see she drinks two or three in a row.''

"You've done this before?''

"Something like it, Eli. With my other dueña, the one who was killed when the Apaches took me. During siesta in the afternoons, I would get her a doctored drink that would put her to sleep. Then I could sneak out and go swimming and spy on the boys playing naked in the water. It's a good thing I had nothing on either those times or it would have made a terrible mess in my undergarments. Tia Alicia would have found out and known I was having," Esmeralda demurely lowered her eyelids, "impure thoughts.''

"Your thoughts right now are impure enough. They're having an effect on me," Eli informed

148

her, squirming slightly at the sudden swell in his tight trousers.

Esmeralda brightened. "Oh. Good then. We'll go ahead. Get her drunk and then we can use the little room off the back stairs."

"I, ah, all right, give it a try," Eli responded, driven by his own urgent need.

Machismo demanded it, and his wounded pride goaded Fidel Ocampo into the brash move. Dressed in his finest, freshly shaved and his mustache trimmed to a pencil line, Fidel Ocampo mingled with the guests at the fiesta. A relative stranger to these parts, he felt confident no one would recognize him. The general mood on such an evening aided him in his masquerade. He ate and drank with the crowd and watched everything intently. Among the things he noted was an old cannon, obviously useless now, standing near the front door to the main house.

He also saw his nemisis, the tall, blond gringo. He watched with tightly controlled fury as the gringo and an aristocratic young woman slipped away from the whirl of dancers and darted hand-in-hand down an empty corridor. El Gallo followed moments later. He abruptly pulled back into shadow when they paused at a low, narrow doorway and looked back along the hall. The latch clicked loudly and they entered, securing the door behind them. Ocampo hurried forward and listened. Voices came from within.

"Hurry, dearest, get me out of this dress," Esmeralda pleaded. "I'm fainting away with desire."

"I'm sort of clumsy at buttons," the deep baratone voice of the scout responded.

"Something new you've been afflicted with?" Esmeralda teased. "Oh, do hurry, Eli."

Smiling broadly, Fidel Ocampo mentally located this room in his diagram of the hacienda he carried in memory. Satisfied, he found the nearest door leading to the outside and slipped through it. A rose trellis led upward to the tall, narrow, barred window. El Gallo climbed it with cautious ease. The sash had been swung open and he could hear and see the action below.

Naked to the waist, Eli Holten embraced Esmeralda Escobar. She wore only a tight band around her chest as custom demanded and a thin shift. Dress and petticoats lay scattered around her. They kissed long and heatedly. El Gallo looked on and grew uncomfortable. Eli's fingers untied the band and freed her breasts. El Gallo stifled a groan.

As Esmeralda undid the scout's trousers, El Gallo felt a tightness in his loins.

"Now, beloved. Hurry, take me, take me," she gasped.

Eli lifted her into his arms and strode to the bed. There he took her in wild abandon. El Gallo began to tremble.

"This . . . is sort of . . . by way . . . of farewell," Eli panted, as their bodies melded into one.

"Wha-what do you mean, Eli?"

"I . . . we're . . . leaving tomorrow morning, Esmeralda," the scout answered.

Their rocking motion grew more frenzied. El Gallo shook like the last leaf of summer in a gale. Esmeralda made little cooing sounds and flung her head from side to side in rhythm with Eli's masterful strokes.

"You don't . . . have to . . . go," Esmeralda rallied

to say. "Poppa . . . would be . . . pleased to see . . . us married."

"Later. We'll talk about it later," Eli pleaded. "Right now . . . I want . . . I-I-I-I . . ."

Release came at once to Esmeralda as well. Likewise to Fidel Ocampo.

Swiftly he climbed down the trellis, made his way to his horse and slipped off into the night. He had seen enough, Fidel convinced himself. He had also done a more daring thing than any of those gringo ladrones would ever try.

Back in the small room another energetic bout of love began.

Daybreak brought a bustle of activity to the Casa Escobar. Barefoot servants hurried to saddle horses. In the atrium of the main house, Eli Holten and his men sat at a large table with their host and Esmeralda Escobar. They enjoyed the cool air and clear, blue sky above. Chocolate and herb tea had been served and off in the detached cooking wing the odors of a magnificent breakfast wafted out on the slight breeze.

"There is no need for you to make so hasty a departure, Don Eli," Don Francisco urged on his friend. "What is another day or a week?"

"I have my obligations to our country's Army, Don Francisco," Eli answered vaguely. His body still hummed from the ardor of last night's lovemaking.

"If they gave you indefinite leave, then shouldn't you take full advantage of it?" his host suggested.

"I feel I already have. It's over a month since we left Globe. General Crook will think I met my end at the hands of bandits," Eli argued.

Don Francisco shrugged and gestured grandly,

151

palms upraised before him. "Ah, in my youth, I, too, had such devotion to duty. It's a mark of aging that one finds urgent affairs are often able to work themselves out over the long term, rather than the short. Ah! Here comes Maria with our first course.

A short, stout woman in colorfully embroidered white dress with puff sleeves bore a large platter of assorted fruit to the table. Everyone helped themselves and fell to silently eating. A basket of hot bread rolls came a short time later. Through the entire breaking of their fast, Esmeralda Escobar kept her leg pressed firmly against that of Eli Holten. Her eyes held a dreamy, far away look.

"So all of you know how we're going to do this, I want you to listen closely," T. Luther Hayden said loudly to the gathered outlaws. "We'll attack in two elements, from the east and the south, at the same time. The idea is to strike so fast that we get in among the buildings of the *estancia* before there is time to organize a defense. Until we join up with El Gallo, Señor Beltran here will lead his forces. Jake, you'll take the right flank and I'll have the left. Likewise, Señor Beltran will take the left during the attack and El Gallo will be closest to me. What's the count, Jake?"

"There's forty-one of us and twenty-five of the Mez—ah, El Gallo's men," the huge black informed his leader.

"See this is translated to our friends," T. Luther instructed. "Gentlemen, by nightfall today, we shall command an empire that will stretch from this valley, eastward across the mountains and the central plain to the Sierra Madre Oriental. Each man will be the captain of his own town. Not even the government of Mexico will dare to challenge us!"

A lusty cheer broke out.

Although he felt the importance of an early start, Eli Holten found himself lingering over a cigar with his host. Don Francisco used all his charm to attempt to keep the fighting men at his hacienda. One never knew when their skills might be needed against the dread Yaquis or the numerous bandits who roamed the mountains to the east. At last, Eli rose and walked toward the tunnel-like passage to the front gate.

"We can wait no longer, Don Francisco. It has been a delightful interlude and a profitable one for us, thanks to your generosity. The mails are unreliable at best, though I promise you I'll try to keep in touch."

"We are poorer for your departure. With what I have bestowed, each of you could become a gentleman of leisure here in Sonora. A few head of cattle and some land would make you one of our class and persons of importance. Think it over, amigo mio."

"I have," Eli said with a trace of regret. "And that youthful sense of duty still prevails. Good-bye, Don Francisco." He paused and looked for Esmeralda. "Where's Esmeralda? I wanted to say farewell."

"She was taken with womanly tears and hurried off while you were loading your personal items," Don Francisco informed Eli. "I think you can look up and will find her on the little balcony outside her room."

Eli stepped to his Morgan stallion and turned back, glancing upward. Esmeralda waved a small lace handkerchief and fought back tears. "Good-bye, my hero Eli," she called in a tiny voice.

"Good-bye, Esmeralda. I shall miss your company."

"Vaya con dios, Señores," Don Francisco heartily wished them.

Up in their saddles, the small contingent of Americans turned their horses' heads toward the wide, arched adobe gateway that marked the outer wall of the estate. Before Eli and his men reached it a waving peon stiffened suddenly and pitched face first onto the ground. The crack of a rifle shot followed instantly.

Shouting and howling, weapons ablaze, the combined force of El Gallo's bandidos and the American hardcases launched their attack.

"Shut those gates!" Eli Holten shouted as he reined in.

Swiftly dismounting, Eli slid his Winchester from the saddle scabbard and opened fire on the wide front of charging riders. Two more peons went down before one side of the wrought iron gate slammed into place. The other had six feet to go, the men pushing it cringed low in an attempt to dodge bullets. Three attackers made it inside.

Eli downed one, then a second with well-aimed shots from his Winchester. The third whirled to fire at the peasants shoving the gate. A loud boom from behind drew Eli's attention as the bandit slumped forward in the saddle, a blood-seeping hole in the back of his embroidered jacket.

Don Francisco still held the huge .60-90-750 breech loader of Spanish design to his shoulder while smoke coiled around him. He lowered it and turned to shout orders to his *vaqueros*.

"Get to your horses. Have no mercy on these ladrónes! Hurry men," the gray haired gentleman bellowed. Automatically he opened the trapdoor breech and extracted the spent cartridge. Another lead-tipped brass cylinder replaced it. Taking quick aim, Don Francisco fired again.

Eli produced a brief smile and turned back to the fray. Already the wide front of the charge had begun to condense into a hard-riding column of fours, boring in on the unsecured gate. They could easily push it aside and storm the grounds. To either side, Eli noted the rest of his small band spread out, placing carefully aimed fire among the attackers. Two men fell from their saddles and the charge faltered. A nagging thought formed into an idea and Eli hurried back to the front of the hacienda.

"Does that cannon work?" he demanded of Don Francisco.

"Of course. I make sure it's always in good order."

"Send someone to the blacksmiths for a keg of nails, where's the powder?"

Realization dawned. "Oh-ho, I see you have an unpleasant surprise for our foe, no? That small structure, the one that looks like a dog house. My powder magazine."

Eli hurried to obtain the necessary elements. More of the *vaqueros* and craftsmen of the *estancia* had rallied now and slowed the charge short of the gateway. Eli dumped what he estimated to be a pound and half of coarse-grain powder down the muzzle and used a greasy ball of uncombed cotton for a wad. A lad of twelve or so showed up with a small keg of nails. Fighting time and a premonition that all would be in vain, Eli smashed the end and began to stuff nails down the tube. With a bit over five pounds of nasty projectiles inserted, he added another wad and took time to light a cigar. Hurriedly

155

he puffed it to a glowing tip.

"Everyone out of the way," Eli yelled to his men and the ranch workers.

"Cool bastard," T. Luther Hayden thought as he watched Eli light his smoke. "Too bad it's a bluff. Ortega assured me that cannon was inoperable."

The last thought came a moment before Eli touch-holed the six pound cannon with the glowing coal of his cigar. Then the world filled with shrieking bits of metal, the cannon's mouth belching flame, smoke and nails.

CHAPTER 15

Shrieking like condemned souls in hell, horses reared and unseated their riders, men howled in torment among the front three ranks of advancing bandits. Those not killed outright were hacked and stabbed by the flying nails. At once the charge ended and mass, panicked retreat took its place.

"The gates! Secure the gates!" Eli Holten yelled over the tumult.

Four of Don Francisco's men rushed to do so. Eli seemed to be everywhere. Sonny snorted through his red-lined black nose and plunged from place to place while Eli organized a defense. "Pull some wagons across that gate. Get everyone inside," he commanded.

"They're stopping, about a thousand paces from the wall," called a lookout on the rooftop of the hacienda.

"Hurry up," Eli demanded. "Get inside and seal the smaller gates."

A narrow wooden platform ran around the inside of the low, twelve-foot outer wall. It provided a convenient firing position. From the arms room in the main house, Don Francisco issued his men with rifles and cartridges. To some went bags of balls, powder horns and percussion caps. The old gentleman stooped and exerted all his strength to drag out two large wooden boxes. From these he handed out spherical metal cannisters with fuse protruding from the top of each.

"These I usually save for the Yaquis. They're quite useful. Some of my people have become competent grenadiers," he explained to Eli. "Yes, you, too, Pepe," he told a lad of about thirteen.

Grinning broadly the boy scampered away clutching five of the deadly bombs. Don Francisco's face took on a gentle expression. "Pepe's like my own sons, before they grew up and married. But he's brave and an accurate thrower. I have some other nasty surprises for these *ladrones*. There are two more cannon, concealed in revetments atop the house. This one we'll wheel out to the gate and load with musket balls."

"You've a-ah, quite formidable defense, Don Francisco," Eli observed.

"And why not? For many years the casa grande was the only outpost of civilization in this valley. My father defended it, as I have, against all sorts of attacks. We became rather adept at it, don't you think?"

"I'd say you could do rather well. So long, at least, that those men don't breech the walls."

"Those walls were built to stand off attacks by Apaches, Yaquis and bandits, Don Eli," Don Francisco explained. "They have served well for nearly a hundred years."

"There appeared to be a large number of whitemen among those bandits," Eli pointed out. "They tend to fight a good deal differently than Indians or bandidos."

*   *   *

T. Luther Hayden's stomach roiled, sour and burning from his unexpected defeat. He slammed a clenched fist down on the horn of his saddle. Now they would have to do it the hard way.

"Bring the Gatling gun up here," he ordered.

"Them fuckers didn't lose a man that counted," Jake Jackson remarked. "Sheeit, we done got us a siege on our hands."

"Looks that way, Jake," T. Luther agreed. "I should have put more of our men in the lead. They'd not broken at the first setback."

"'Setback?' You' talkin' about flyin' nails, T. Luther. Them Mezkin boys was gettin' chewed up like in a buzz-saw. 'At were more than any li'll ol' 'setback.'"

"Make way, here comes the gun," Grover Hanks yelled.

"Set that thing up and start chewing at those walls. Make them keep their heads down so we can charge again," T. Luther ordered.

Unlimbered, the Gatling gun was turned into line. The gun crew swung the pivoting trails wide to provide support. The long, slightly curved, heavy magazine, which held one hundred .45-70 cartridges was hoisted into place. After the crew released the stays so the multiple barrel weapon could traverse, the gunner swung it from side to side taking aim. Satisfied, he set the elevation angle and reached for the crank.

"Open fire," T. Luther ordered.

Metal rattled and clanked for a moment, then the loud reports of discharging .45-70 rounds grew to a roar as the gunner swung to left and right. Bullets began to strike along the top edge of the wall. Men crouched down and cried out in alarm. A mound of bright brass began to rise below the gun.

"Keep it up," T. Luther urged. "Give 'em a good taste of that and see how they act."

"You think they'll give up?" Dave Denton asked.

"They will . . . or die to the last man. We want to make sure they know that."

Eli Holten cursed with hard, purposeful words. "Who'd ever think of them having that?"

"What is it, Don Eli?" Don Francisco asked.

"A Gatling gun. Stolen of course from the U.S. Army. If they have enough ammunition to feed it, they can turn your nice, secure walls into a prison for us. Unless we can take it out with a cannon."

"We can try," Don Francisco offered with a shrug.

On the roof-top, Eli bent low while .45-70 slugs cracked overhead. Neither cannon faced the deadly Gatling. He gave terse directions to Don Francisco, who informed his men what to do. Slowly one of the five hundred pound tubes and its clumsy carriage came free of its position and the men strained on their knees to put it in place. Not a one dared to stand. The slightest show of movement brought an immediate rain of hot lead. Sitting down the hacienda gunners heaved to the point of hernias to move the massive piece.

At last it came to rest, muzzle rearing over the parapet, pointed generally toward the Gatling gun. For a moment, no one did a thing.

"Use the sight, Ramon," Don Francisco suggested gently.

Ramon Garcia risked his life to rise up enough to insert the bore sight into the maw of the gun. He squinted through the subjective lens and waved a hand to instruct the gunners.

"To the right. More. More. There, that's it. Right

160

in line. Now up. Turn the elevating screw."

Slowly the muzzle rose. Two diameters . . . three . . . five . . . "A little more," Ramon asked. "Hold it."

He turned back to Don Francisco and plopped on his rump a moment before a bullet cracked through the space his chest formerly occupied. "You may load and fire, *patron*."

"You heard him," Don Francisco told the others. "Pull it back, load and make ready to fire."

Clumsily, from lack of steady practice, although with a ready will, the gunners complied. They leaned into the ropes to pull the gun into firing position. Then Ramon took one side of the cannon, Eli the other.

"You may fire when ready," Ramon said.

A terrible blast followed, its thunder rumbling over the hills and off the distant mountains. Eli instinctively blinked, then caught sight of the black dot that was the projectile. He watched it sail through the air in what appeared a slow, lazy arc. It landed with a splash of dirt and sand, and a moment later exploded in a loud, sharp crack.

"Short," Ramon called out. "Up three, right one. Fire again."

Laboriously the cannon was adjusted, swabbed out and reloaded. Smoke flashed from the touch hole and another awful flat blam sounded.

"Short by one and a half," Raul sang out. "Next time we get them."

"By God, they've got a cannon up there, too," one of the American adventurers shouted when the first round fired.

"They're shootin' at us," the gunner announced

161

nervously when the ball burst to the left of his muzzles, four hundred yards short.

"Make it hot for them," T. Luther shouted. "Keep their heads down."

The Gatling gun roared until heat and powder fouling jammed it. "Quick, flush it out," the gunner yelled, yanking the magazine free.

Clear water sizzled on the hot metal and a thick, black liquid ran off from the bottom of the gun. More water flowed and foamed until the outpour turned a milky gray. In the distance the cannon boomed again. The gunner inserted the magazine in the top of the gun and reached for the crank.

Ear piercing noise came when the shell exploded less than a hundred yards in front of the gun. A shower of dust and fragments of metal rained on the men manning the Gatling.

"I'm hit," one man cried out.

"Get a replacement up here," T. Luther commanded. "Keep firing."

"We better pull back. They're getting our range," the gunner suggested.

"Shoot until you jam again," T. Luther demanded. "Then pull back."

"That might be too damn late," the gunner objected.

"Do it, or I'll shoot you where you stand," T. Luther's voice turned to ice.

Resignedly the gunner reached for his crank.

"Over one," Ramon called.

In the distance, Eli Holten could see the Gatling gun crew limbering up their weapon and hurrying it to the rear. A stocky man on a gray horse appeared to be yelling imprecations at them.

"I think we've made them turn tail with that Gatling gun," Eli observed dryly. "They're off for the other side of the hill."

"Cease firing, Ramon. We are short on powder," Don Francisco advised.

"*Sí, patron.*"

"Come, Don Eli. Let us see how we fare elsewhere," the old man said calmly as though he suggested a stroll in the park.

"It's fortunate you planned another fiesta, Don Francisco," Eli observed as they came down from the room and walked past the detached kitchen building.

"Yes, we have ample food for a siege. If only someone gets word out to the army. Not all of the *vaqueros* could have been taken without a fight. We would have heard shooting to warn us."

Eli declined comment. It seemed more likely to him that when none of the *vaqueros* on patrol fired a shot or appeared at the hacienda ahead of the attackers they wouldn't be coming in and hadn't gone for help. Whatever the case, Eli believed they were in a situation only they could do something about.

"Our big problem is ammunition," Don Francisco went on. "Once my men begin firing, it's hard to make them stop. That consumes a lot of cartridges uselessly."

"Perhaps my men can help in that," Eli offered. "Teach them fire discipline."

"Eh? How is that?"

"Teach them to stop firing where there's nothing to shoot at, Don Francisco. Their methods may be a little rough, put a few lumps on some of your *campasinos'* heads, but in the end they'll be good as regulars."

Don Francisco smiled bleakly. "For which I will be

eternally grateful. See what you can do."

"I will at the next opportunity," Eli promised.

That came sooner than Eli expected. While he explained the problem to Carlos O'Banyon and Ed Hendrickson, the Gatling gun opened fire from another direction and using its covering fire a swarm of yelling bandits descended on the hacienda.

Fidel Ocampo rode in the lead of his shouting, firing bandit gang as they zig-zagged down the low hillside toward the walls of the hacienda. One by one he counted the puffs as rifle fire opened against them. There must be twenty men on the outer wall. From close at hand he heard the familiar "hun-hun-hun," like a chant.

Poor Ojo Beltran. Since boyhood he had been terrified of horses. He stuck to them, though, holding the saddle horn and quaking with fear. No man had ever faced down Fidel's closest friend, yet the face of a horse poked close to him day or night could send him screaming. Fidel glanced El Ojo's way to give him assurance and turned back in time to see the center wagon rolled away from the gate. Were they giving up?

The black snout of the cannon waiting there belched a flaming negative reply to Fidel's question. Men and animals shrieked in pain and a whole rank went down like a windrow of grain. *Jésus, Maria y Jóse*, how had he been missed?

Jóse Garza had not been so fortunate. For a fleeting moment he turned a shock-and-pain numbed face toward his leader. Two nails protruded half their length from his forehead, a third from an eyesocket and two more poked from his throat. He wavered briefly in his saddle and fell away to roll in the dust.

"Turn away! Turn away! Take the other wall!" El Gallo commanded.

Tactically it was a mistake. The cannon could not be reloaded before they swarmed over the gate and tore it open. This provided time for the defenders to rally and switch their strength to the threatened spot.

Fully thirty rifles spouted smoke at them when the bandits swung in toward the southern wall. A small boy stood up and hurled a round, dark object. It landed near Lupe Ybarra's mount and exploded with a thunderous roar. The horse's head flew one direction, one forequarter another, while Lupe, punctured in a dozen places by shrapnel, howled his life away as he bled profusely. Another shriek of terror rose from the scene as the flying head struck El Ojo Beltran on the shoulder.

Eyes wide and showing only white, El Ojo reined around and streaked away cross the open ground, spurs shredding his mount's flanks. Sick at heart, with grenades exploding all around, El Gallo had but one choice.

"Turn back! Fall back, amigos! Run for the hills!"

CHAPTER 16

Not mournful dove nor cheerful songbird roosted at Rancho Fortunado. Only the disapproving cluck of hens and prideful crow of roosters could be heard. Tempers had grown short during the three days of the siege, as had ammunition. Eli Holten spent much of his time overseeing the distribution of cartridges, powder and shot. Don Francisco had given Eli the keys to the stores when the exigencies of age limited the older man's participation in the fighting. Early on the fourth morning, Carlos O'Banyon came to the armory to receive his twenty rounds.

"What gets me is that no one has come to our aid," the cocky Irish-Mexican remarked.

"Which tells me that no one got away to go for help," Eli remarked.

"I'm afraid you're right. Tell me, how long do you think we can hold out?"

Eli considered the question. He'd asked himself often enough. "A little longer than the bandits can afford to stay here attacking us, I think."

O'Banyon frowned. "How's that?"

"Some of the guests are expected back at their ranches or to businesses in towns. When they don't show up, it's likely someone will come looking. That

167

should bring troops here in short order."

"I'll be happy to see that, if and when it comes." O'Banyon's mood changed. "I'm the last, so you can lock up and go get some breakfast, lad."

"None too soon," Eli admitted. "After a night without a single alarm, I'm fairly sure the bandits are up to something. No telling when it might start."

"That's right," T. Luther Hayden assured the mixed bag of outlaws. "Put the scaling ladders here on the back slope. They're out of sight of the hacienda, as you will be."

"Are you sure there is no other way?" Fidel Ocampo asked him.

"Certain enough," T. Luther responded. "They have to be running low on ammunition. And they've lost a few men. You noticed, didn't you, in our last foray that they couldn't put an adequate force on every wall at the same time. All we should need to do is launch a diversionary attack with mounted men, get them fully engaged. Then, when their concentration is fixed on the wrong place, the ladders go forward, our men climb the wall and it's over in a few minutes."

"Won't they be able to change their defenses?"

"Nope. The ladders will be carried by men on horseback. The rest will run along side and throw them up against the wall the moment they get there. We'll have the Gatling gun in position to keep the top of the wall along here free of effective defenders. It will stop firing when the men start up the ladders."

"It appears you have thought of everything," Fidel Ocampo remarked sincerely.

"Thank you, El Gallo," T. Luther responded,

168

puffing with pride. "Just make certain everyone does his part so that it works."

Clanging discordantly, the bell of the small church began to ring the moment riders appeared along the ridge to the north of the hacienda. Reinforcements rushed there as the bandits charged down on the beleagered defenders. On the rooftop of the main house, men struggled to horse a cannon around to provide long-range fire.

"They've not hit from this side before," Eli observed. "Wonder what changed their minds?"

Eli and two of his men answered the alarm. That left only two in charge of the remaining defenses. The outlaws drew considerably closer without firing, Eli noted. No doubt they, too, had gotten low on ammunition. Something new had been added, he observed when thin sputters of smoke rose from the hands of several attackers. A volley of fire came from the bandits and those with the sparkling objects rode in closer. Dynamite!

"Shoot for the riders in close. They've got dynamite bombs," Eli called out a moment before the first bundle was thrown.

At the same moment, on the far side of the compound, the staccato *thump-thump-thump* of the Gatling gun opened up. A two sided attack? Damn, they hadn't the resources to properly counter that, Eli thought in desperation. At least Carlos O'Banyon commanded that south wall. He had a cool head and a practiced eye. Perhaps that long-barreled Express Rifle Carlos acquired when John Oates died could take out the gunners. A loud blast went off three foot short of the top wall.

The force knocked several men flat. Unharmed, they came up lusting for blood. Eli noted that Ed Hendrickson was putting his own long range rifle to use. On the brow of the hill sat two men, obviously commanding the attack. Ed took aim and squeezed off a round.

At six hundred yards, time lag was several noticeable heartbeats long. Even Eli Holten, with all his experience, began to wonder if it had been a miss by the time one of the horses made an exaggerated flinch and then folded in the forequarters. The rider, dressed in a short jacket and broad-brimmed sombrero, kicked free of the stirrups and scurried away on all fours before the beast collapsed to the hard soil.

"Damn, I meant that for the man," Hendrickson swore.

"Good shooting anyway, Ed. Mightuv put the fear of the Almighty in him," Eli responded.

"It'll take more than that to stop these bastards," Hendrickson growled.

"I am unharmed, amigo, but I need another horse," Fidel Ocampo yelled from behind the crest.

"The scaling ladders should be in place," T. Luther Hayden observed. "We need to press the attack harder here."

"I'll see to it," El Gallo assured him. He signaled the small reserve and with them, remounted now, raced down the hill to press the enemy harder.

"Keep going! Keep running! Keep up with the rest!" Jake Jackson bellowed at the lagging men among the scaling force.

Most of the ladders had reached the wall with minimal resistance and not a casualty. They began to go up when Jackson heard the crack of a heavy bullet over his head. A moment later came the whining *wow* when the slug richocheted off the top of the barrel assembly of the Gatling gun. He looked upward for the sharpshooter.

"Arriba-arriba!" El Ojo screamed at his men as they began ascending the first ladders.

Brown-skinned men swarmed at the bases of the hand-made climbing rings. Some began to ascend. There came the hollow boom of an eight gauge shotgun and three men fell away from the first ladder. There, Jackson chose rightly, standing between those two ladders. The short one. He fired another blast with his shotgun and then picked up a long Express Rifle. Despite the bullets whizzing around him, he took careful aim and fired the big weapon. Jackson discharged his sixgun at the same time.

His bullet smacked into the floor plate of the Express. Impact drove Carlos O'Banyon's thumb into his eye socket. Pain from the cut eyeball blinded Carlos. Blood began to flow and he blinked rapidly in an attempt to clear his vision. His work with the rifle had been well done, though. The gunner of the Gatling lay in a spreading pool of his own gore. Groping sightlessly, Carlos replaced the damaged Express with his eight gauge Parker and fired downward.

Double O pellets splashed ragged holes in the crowns of four men's heads and they fell away from the ladders. The second barrel discharged in time with another shot from Jake Jackson. That slug took Carlos in the left shoulder. Men jostled past the huge

171

black outlaw and flung themselves at the steps that separated them from their enemy. Jackson fired again, while Carlos reloaded.

White agony burned in Carlos O'Banyon's chest. He swayed, weakened by loss of blood. His left eye cleared and he looked down on a grinning black face behind a smoking revolver. With a mighty effort, he snapped closed the breech of the Parker and triggered a round. The rising breeze whipped away the smoke in time for Carlos O'Banyon to see the black face turned into a raw pulp, red as high summer raspberry jam. A sweet smile turned his Irish face pixieish for a moment and he fell dead at the same instant as his killer.

Wreathed in smoke, flame lancing from the muzzle, the rooftop cannon spoke. Nails, bits of broken horseshoes and a handful of precious musket balls flew from its hot breath to slash into the milling bandits who had forced a wedge atop the wall. Shrieking and writhing, more than half their number fell to the narrow platform. The peasants of Don Francisco's rancho flung themselves at the survivors and quickly dispatched them.

"Make way! Get clear there," one of four peons shouted as they climbed to the parapet with a huge copper cauldron. Used for deep frying the hunks of pork that made carnitas, the cauldron radiated high heat. The contents roiled and smoked.

The husky porters went directly to the wall and began to pour the fiery liquid over the side. Screams answered their efforts and they moved slowly along, dispensing more boiling oil. Howls of agony rose from a tumult of dust and panicked men.

"Pull back!" the hastily obeyed order went out. "Get back."

Rifles and shotguns opened up from the wall. Bandits staggered about, clawing at their burned faces and weeping like children. Others ran in short circles, pulling oil-sodden shirts from their scarlet-scarred bodies. Those few in control of their emotions made a determined retreat, walking hurriedly backward and firing wildly to suppress the opposition.

"¡El negro grande es muerto!" the cry went among El Gallo's bandidos. Although acutely color-conscious, the Mexican and mestizo bandits had come to admire the solid, courageous black man.

"Hot damn, I don't know if we'll get them Mezkins to attack again," Jim Simmons remarked to another of Hayden's long riders.

"We'd better do something," Quint Rhalls responded.

From the opposite side of the compound, grenades began to explode and the diversionary attack broke off entirely.

"We've got to find a way of cracking that place," T. Luther Hayden stated with vehemence. "Twenty-five dead in a single attack. At that rate we'll run out of men before they run out of tricks. Anyone have an idea?"

Silent, solemn faces answered him. At last, Fidel Ocampo spoke up. "What about a night attack? There will be no moon tonight. They will think that after we . . . we ran today, we'd not be up to an attack again so soon. In the dark we can get in close before they are aware."

173

"You've a point," T. Luther allowed after a moment's consideration. "Their people have to rest. Most likely they'd have only a few sentries out at night."

"My men are good with their knives. They can slit throats and we'll be inside in no time," El Gallo elaborated. "Then, the small outbuildings can be set afire. In the confusion we will throw open the gates, in rides the rest and the fight is over, *como no?*"

"Yes. I can see where that would work. We'd have to be careful with the fires. If they spread to the large barns and the hacienda . . ." T. Luther paused. "Maybe something could be done to put them further off guard. Let me work on it and we'll meet again in an hour."

Eli Holten sat submerged to his neck in a shallow pond. Situated in a small copse of trees at the convergence of two of the outer walls, it afforded a welcome, if unprecedented privacy in which he luxuriated. The long hours of battle and preparation over the past four days had given him scant opportunity to clean himself, beyond a cursory splashing in a glazed pottery basin in his room. This seemed sheer elegance. He rested his head on a flat rock in the shadow of a large fern and allowed the languidly moving water to ease away the strain.

Suddenly he was disturbed when the foliage parted and revealed Esmeralda, her eyes wide and soft with desire, bosom heaving. "I've come to help you take a bath," she said softly.

Just watching her disrobe made the scout's body respond. He could barely wait to embrace her voluptuous curves.

"*¿Dulcita?* Esmeralda, *¿adonde esta?*"

174

Esmeralda produced a pained expression. "My dueña, as we both know. Think, beloved, for I shall die without your love to fill me."

Quickly the clothing reversed direction and Esmeralda hurried off. Eli stifled a groan and began to soap his chest.

CHAPTER 17

Quail called from the sagebrush and long shadows lay across the late afternoon landscape. A lone rider, carrying a white flag, rode along the road to the main gate in the high outer walls of the hacienda. Not deemed significant enough to sound the alarm, he was challenged verbally and a runner sent to the main house.

"I have come on behalf of the great founder of empires, T. Luther Hayden and his associate, Don Fidel Ocampo," the messenger repeated when Eli Holten and Don Francisco Escobar arrived at the gate. "I am instructed to present to you certain terms."

Although the fellow was dressed expensively in the elaborate costume of a *charro*, and spoke in the lofty terms of a courtier, Don Francisco could see that underneath he was nothing but a second-rate bandit. Anger and disgust filled the noble old gentleman. He made to turn away at the brashness of all this. Eli arrested his movement with a hand on his arm.

"What are those?" the scout growled at the emissary.

"Don Luther, who is soon to be emperor of this part of Mexico, sends his compliments for a contest well fought. As one of his future subjects, he regrets

177

any injuries you may have incurred, Don Francisco, and offers a means by which you might honorably end this conflict."

"We have had emperors before," Don Francisco snapped. "The French sent us one and we put him in front of a firing squad."

"Do not be hasty, Don Francisco." Iron tipped his words. "Don Luther is most generous in what he offers. Listen first. There is no need for enmity to exist between you. All Don Luther wants is for you to turn over to him the gringo lawmen whom you have given shelter. He takes no cause with you, or your guests, only with these craven hired guns. If they are turned out, all the rest of you will be spared and the siege will end."

"These men are under the protection of my roof. It would be dishonorable to . . ."

The messenger held up one hand to silence the old *haciendado*. "You are not the church to give sanctuary to foreign mercenaries, Don Francisco. You have one hour to consider this most generous offer. At the end of that time, I'll return for your answer."

With that, he turned his mount and cantered away.

Word of the terms traveled fast around the *estancia*. Esmeralda burst into the meeting in her father's study with her temper, all too familiar to Eli, in full rage.

"No! You can't do this. I won't let you. It's unthinkable to even sit here and discuss it."

For the first time the traditional sternness of his class arose in Don Francisco. "Daughter, take hold of yourself. This is not a matter open to discussion with

178

the ladies of the household. Go to your room."

Esmeralda stamped her foot. "I will not! I . . . I l-love Eli and I won't let this happen. It's beastly that you would even think about trading his life and those of these other brave men for . . . for what?"

Don Francisco looked a bit embarrassed. "That fellow did make it rather clear this Luther Hayden intends to be overlord of some sort. If we don't fight him now, we may well have to another time. Perhaps my daughter has introduced some wisdom into our deliberations."

"She's only clouded them, sir," Eli countered. "I'm willing to go. It gives us a chance for someone to escape this siege and go for help."

"No, Eli!" Esmeralda pleaded. "It is too dangerous. Oh, why did I ever let you bring me here? There is danger for you everywhere."

"You think fighting the Apaches was any safer?" Eli quipped, his own temper rising. "They must be up to something and want a hostage. I've managed to escape from some far more clever people than these," Eli informed the others recalling to mind some bad times in Sioux and Cheyenne villages and war camps.

"But they're utterly ruthless," Esmeralda protested again.

Ignoring her, Eli addressed his host. "Don Francisco, suppose I offer to go out. We tell them that there are none of the men who came with me alive, except a boy who is not even a lawman. Can't you see that this way we have an ear in their camp, as well, and the siege lines will be behind me with the mountains and rescue not far away."

"I'll go too," Peter Taylor spoke up from the corner of the room.

"No, Peter," Eli said gently. "There's no need for that."

"Yes," the boy challenged hotly. "That makes double the chance of an escape and double the number to hear their real plans. You've got to let me go."

Esmeralda's hands flew to her hair. "Are you all mad? So far, no one is going, now this boy, this *child*, wants to accompany Eli to certain death. *Madre de dios*, give these drawingroom adventurers some benefit of your wisdom. Give them eyes to see what's *really* going to happen."

"I'll give you a solid whack on your nether parts, daughter, if you don't keep out of our deliberations," Don Francisco remarked gently. "These are men's affairs."

"This is madness!" Esmeralda shouted.

"Leave us!" her father blared.

Esmeralda bit back a hot reply and fought tears that filled her eyes. With a small whimper she raised her skirts and hurried from the room.

"Well then, Eli, I begin to see your logic in this," Don Francisco took up without a show of emotion. "Perhaps it has merit enough."

"I'll go with him, then, when the messenger returns?"

"Risky . . . but if anyone can make it work, it's you, Don Eli."

"And I'll go with you," Peter inserted.

"No you'll not," Eli snapped.

"Once we have the gringos we still attack tonight, no?" Fidel Ocampo inquired of T. Luther Hayden.

"A plan such as you suggested takes time to lay

180

out," T. Luther explained. "It must be rehearsed to insure nothing goes wrong. That will take a . . . day or two. And a night to practice as well. All of this must be done out of sight of the opposition. The reason for that is obvious. I am convinced that the American lawmen are behind such spirited defense. When we have them prisoner, it is time to go into the second stage of a classical siege."

"Which is, ah, what?" Fidel inquired.

"Simply to keep the enemy bottled up and worried. Wear them down, break their spirit. Then another major assault on the walls."

El Gallo began to chuckle. "I like that. Oh, how clever were the men who discovered these ways to fight."

"It was used by your famous El Cid, to drive the Moors from Spain," T. Luther said patronizingly.

"It was? How about that?" Fidel Ocampo drew himself up. "The blood of conquistadores runs hotly in our veins. We'll not let you down in the battles to come."

You'd better not, T. Luther Hayden thought hotly.

Five men, including Eli Holten, Peter Taylor, and Roberto Pastore, *segundo* of the ranch, rode out from the hacienda at the appointed time. Eli had agreed to Peter's presence only in that it proved his stipulation that the two of them were all who remained of the Americans. In the distance the gaudily dressed envoy and three men started toward them. They met three hundred yards outside the walls.

"You are prepared to surrender the gringos to us, Don Francisco?"

"I'm here to give myself up in exchange for the

181

safety of Don Francisco's ranch and all who live here."

Felipe Torres, the envoy, tightened his expression and his eyes narrowed. "Where are the rest of the gringos?"

"There are none. Except this one, and you can see he is but a boy and no harm to you. The others are dead in the fighting," Eli answered.

It could be true, Torres thought, we know for certain of one, who died in the scaling attempt. "This is a true thing, Don Francisco?"

The old man scowled a moment then snapped, "It is."

"Then we'll take you, the both of you, back to Don Luther and let him decide if the boy is to go free, no?"

"No!" Eli barked. "I'll not allow that."

"There's little you are in a position to allow or disallow, Señor," Torres told the scout sneeringly.

Damn. He'd been foolish to allow Peter to come along to the parlay. Eli cast a glance at the youth, only to see a certain eagerness in Peter's expression. "This ends the siege?"

"That is what has been said by Don Luther," Torres acknowledged blank faced.

"All right. Then . . . we'll go."

The riders with Torres came forward and surrounded Eli and Peter. Silently they started off toward the bandit lines. Felipe Torres made an elaborate saluting gesture with his sombrero and returned it to his head.

"*Vaya con dios*, Don Francisco," he said with a smirk.

Out of sight of the hacienda, the pretense at courtly

conduct ended abruptly. The escort halted Eli Holten and Peter Taylor and bound their hands behind them, removing their arms from saddle and holster. Then a fist smashed into Eli's left kidney. Air exploded from his lungs in a soft wheeze and black snowflakes danced before his eyes. Sagging he slumped off onto the ground.

"Gringo peeg!" the beefy one who had struck him spat. "Stan' up and' walk, *cabrón*."

"I—I c-can't," Eli gasped. Pain in the small of his back made his legs watery. He could force himself if need be, but wanted to test the severity of his captors at the outset.

The dandified one caught up and dismounted. Taking Eli by the shoulders he raised him to his feet. "Let me help you, Señor. You have been a gallant enemy."

Neither T. Luther Hayden nor any of his fellow bandidos knew that Felipe Torres was not only literate but had spent his boyhood reading the romantic adventures of the days when knighthood was in flower. Picked to play the role of a feudal herald, he had fallen into it completely. At least, as regarded the treatment of prisoners or hostages.

"Thank you, ah . . ." Eli prompted.

"Felipe Torres, at your service, Señor."

"Thank you, Don Felipe. You do your *patrón* honor," Eli asserted with a certain sincerity.

Flattered at being called sir, Felipe bent to dust off Eli's jacket and trousers. Holten noted the reaction and the look in the bandit's eyes. That he might profitably use later on. Torres then aided him to mount again.

"It is not much farther, Señor. Then Don Luther has some questions for you."

183

"I'm sure he does," Eli answered wearily.

"You expect me to believe that you two are all that's left?" T. Luther Hayden demanded some twenty minutes later.

"I do, because that's the truth," Eli staunchly told him.

"I could turn you over to El Gallo's bandidos. They're more Indian than Mexican and have some interesting ways of getting answers."

"Do what pleases you," Eli said with a lightness he definitely did not feel. "I've told you the truth. I'm a scout on General Crook's staff, the others were men I hired to help me escort Senorita Escobar back to her family. None of us are lawmen or bounty hunters and don't give a damn if you conquer all of Mexico. All we wanted to do was go home, then you attacked. That hardly puts us in a mood of overwhelming gratitude to you."

"I'm sure that it wouldn't," T. Luther admitted, evincing his first grudging credence in their story. "The point is, we're going to take that hacienda and we're going to hold you until we do. We can't be held responsible in the states for what we do down here. Once we've established our little empire, perhaps we can look into letting you go. Until then you'll be given a place to sleep and to eat, and guarded closely. Henderson," he went on, raising his voice. "Take these men to that tent under the cottonwood. See they have water and feed them at mealtime. Fix 'em up with leg shackles but free their hands until lights out."

"Right away, Boss," Henderson agreed.

Once left on their own, Peter turned to Eli. "What

184

do we do now?''

"We start fixing it so that *I* can escape from here."

"Why can't we both go?" Peter asked with a pout.

"Better chance of success with only one," Eli told him. "Everyone, even the best, makes some sound when moving around. It might seem funny, but two people make three times as much noise as one alone. I know where they put Sonny. He's trained and won't do anything to alert them. I can take him, walk away a distance and be off from here long before they know I'm gone. It can't be too far to find help and I'll be back before they can do something drastic."

"What can I do?" ever-eager Peter asked.

Eli seated himself on the dirt floor. They had a table and two crude camp chairs, none of which would do any good at this point. Eli stretched out his legs.

"Are you any good at picking locks?"

Peter gave him a sly look. "I, uh, well, I've, ah, done it a couple of times."

"On your father's liquor supply, perhaps?" Eli's eyes twinkled with merriment.

"Uh, yeah. And his gun rack. He was gone for a while and I wanted to go shoot some rabbits, or a deer. Something to eat besides salt pork."

"Give these a try," Eli suggested, gesturing to his leg irons.

After several futile attempts, Peter removed his belt and bent the metal tongue. This he inserted into the lock plate and held it in place with a wedge of broken button. Sweat dotting his upper lip, he gently rotated the makeshift pick. Several false starts followed, then a grating sound and sharp click rewarded his efforts.

"I did it!" he declared excitedly.

"Peter, hush!" the scout hissed. "Good for us that river out there's so loud over the rocks."

"They've all gone off somewhere," Peter returned defensively.

"To take a few shots at the hacienda. But you can be sure not all of them. They'd not chance leaving us alone. Now undo the other side."

It more effort than the first. Twice the improvised key slipped. At last the tumblers threw and Eli removed the shackles.

"Good work, Peter. Now lock them and see if you can open them again."

"D'you mean on you?"

"No. I want to see if it can be done before we take that chance," Eli informed him.

Peter locked them easily enough. Then, while attempting to open the first lock, the button broke. Although he tried all the others on his shirt, he could not get one the exact size to serve as a lever. Two fragments wedged together were also a failure.

"Well, that decides it. I go now. Out the back of the tent," Eli announced.

"If they bring something to eat, you'll be found out too soon," Peter cautioned.

"I doubt that'll happen until that Hayden feller, or Torres comes back," Eli opined. In the distance they could faintly hear gunshots over the river's burble.

"Good luck, Eli," Peter offered, somewhat choked up.

"You're a good man, Peter," Eli responded.

With that, he slipped out into the silence of the camp. Two supposed guards snored in the shade of some rocks and a smaller tree. Long shadows, from the impending twilight lay across the ground between the tent and the horse picket line. With all

186

the skill of a Sioux warrior, Eli used them to move unseen to where Sonny waited, head down, dozing.

Eli held the bridle. "No time for a saddle, old Son. We'll just slip out of here, quiet-like, what say?"

In moments, man and horse disappeared in the knee-deep river.

CHAPTER 18

Seemingly fearful of plunging into the waters of the Pacific Ocean, the sun lingered far off in the west. T. Luther Hayden gave full measure of his fury when Eli Holten was discovered to be missing. With one hand he yanked Peter Taylor off the ground and shook him violently.

"Where did he go?" the outlaw leader demanded.

"B-back to the hacienda," Peter lied artfully.

"Oh? Why didn't he take you?"

"Said I'd be too noisy."

T. Luther backhanded Peter, snapping his head from side to side for several moments. "You're lying."

"No!" Peter shouted. "No, I'm not. He knew that you had lied about stopping the siege and he had to go back and help them."

"How noble. Yet he abandoned you?" T. Luther sneered. "Even a cretin like you should see the inconsistency."

"It's the truth," Peter insisted. "They have lots of ammunition and plenty of powder for the three cannons. Mr. Holten said they could hold out long enough."

"Help can't be more than a day's ride away and he chooses to go back? I don't believe you, boy. There are ways of finding out how truthful you are." T. Luther turned to one of his henchmen. "Take him out and tie his legs together with a long coil of rope. Get someone with a horse used to pulling things. A little ride around camp ought to improve his truthfulness."

"On a reverse slope in the first line of foothills, less than half a mile from the camp, Eli Holten crouched in the sparse vegetation and peered over the ridge at the leisurely lowering sun. Below he saw activity in the camp and accurately discerned that his absence had been discovered. After a short while, two burly white men dragged a slight form from the tent. It could only be Peter, Eli realized. What would they do?

While he watched, they rigged Peter to a drag rope. Anger began to rise in the scout at his helpless position. T. Luther Hayden appeared and gave a curt signal. The mounted man dragged Peter once around the camp. T. Luther bent low over the battered figure and appeared to speak. Whatever answer he received failed to satisfy him. The outlaw leader signaled for another round.

Almost the scout could hear Peter's howls of agony as the pace increased this time. In his mind he heard them only too well and a bitter bile rose in his throat. His heart ached. Nothing had indicated that such a thing would be done. Hayden and his pretenses to empire seemed a bit mad, yet gave no hint of such brutality. Ocampo and his bandits, perhaps. They knew and used the harshest measures to keep entire villages in line and paying tribute. Cursing under his breath, Eli fixed his eyes on the unspeakable cruelty.

Unable to help, Eli found himself equally unable to leave his vantage point until the bloody deed had played to an end. Not a religious man, Eli Holten nevertheless offered up a white man's prayer he'd learned in childhood and one to the Sioux Keeper of the Afterworld for the repose of Peter Taylor's spirit, before he sadly crawled away, mounted Sonny and rode off into the gathering night.

Stars alone did not provide enough light for Eli Holten to read the face of his big turnip watch. From the positions of the constellations he gauged it to be shortly after midnight. He had come a far ways and detected no sign of pursuit. Faithful Peter had kept his silence apparently. Even that reflection failed to raise the scout's spirits. He would push on, he decided, until the steep mountain sides made it too dark to go further.

Half a mile along the road to San Patricio de las Palmas, two squat, bulky shapes rose from the scrub along the verge and stood menacingly, with rifles ready. Holten reined in and raised empty hands. Grunts and an impatient gesture with the muzzle of a Springfield carbine showed Eli the way. One of his captors took the reins. A hundred paces off the trail, in a fold of the mountain, they stopped. After a whispered exchange, the scout was pulled from Sonny's back.

Swiftly the burly men secured his hands and pushed him toward a low, crudely made wikiup. The only light showed dimly from inside. A hard hand bent his head and he was propelled into the rude structure.

"You were foolish to come this way . . . and alone," Dos-Tan-Nanta said in Athapascan dialect of the Apache people.

"Red Head," Eli Holten said levelly. "I'm surprised to find you still in Mexico."

"We have long memories. You are the scout called Sharp Eye by the traitor Ski-Be-Nan-Ted?"

"I am," Eli allowed.

"You are a brave man. Why do you come this way in the night?" Red Head inquired.

Slowly, in his incomplete Apache, Eli explained the attack on the hacienda. Familiar now with the customs of these people, he played down his part in the siege and spoke only of the plight of the Escobar family and their guests. In particular he dwelled on the Mexican bandits and their participation.

"These are the men who hunt Apache women and children for the scalp bounty. Men without honor."

"And what would you do with them?" Red Head asked bluntly.

"I would go for help, bring the soldiers of Mexico and have them destroy all the bandits, white-eye and Mexican," Eli answered straightly.

"I say we kill him now," one of the reservation-jumpers growled.

"He does us no harm in what he's doing now," Red Head observed.

"I heard a note of sorrow when he spoke of the boy, killed by the bandidos," Alchise put in. "In this, is he not like us?"

"He would bring the soldiers to attack us first," persisted the hold-out.

"Not so," Eli answered for himself. "We're both in a land foreign to us. When we fought, we did so with no loss of honor for either side. I hold no cause with you."

A long silence followed. Then Red Head stirred himself and extended his arm toward the captive. "Unbind him. We have no cause with him, either. You would do this as you say?" he directed to Eli. "In part you would get revenge for our people."

192

"I know that," Eli answered soberly. "That is as it should be."

"How is this so?" the doubter goaded.

Eli thought it over carefully. "If you let me go on my way, and my friends and the Mexicans are rescued, we are all in your debt. If in so doing, we harm your enemies, the debt is canceled. All is as it was before."

"That's wise counsel," Red Head agreed. "Go then, find the help your people need. We will not step in your way."

With strident insistence a rooster crowed on the outskirts of San Patricio de las Palmas. Only the thinnest white line showed on the eastern panorama of sawtoothed mountains. Flickering votive candles and a single kerosene lamp illuminated the interior of the church, where Padre Gustavo went about preparations for the morning Mass. Another lamp glowed in the office of the newly appointed *alguacil*. The lawman, red-eyed and raspy-voiced, had completed a detailed description of what had happened when the gringo bandits had taken over the town. Listening to him was Capt. Gueljermo Sandoval of the Federales detachment located in Hermosillo.

"You say they joined forces with that *payaso* El Gallo Ocampo?" Sandoval asked, incredulous.

"That is true, Capítan," Curro Morales replied. Then he shrugged. "But then, they are gringos, no?"

"Any idea where they went from here?" Sandoval pressed.

"No, Capítan. It's evident they had some big plan in mind. They even left the women alone for a whole day before they departed."

"I gather that they had not been paying for the

women's favors?" At Morales' negative head-shake, Sandoval went on. "Why is it that this kind, ours, the *Norteños*, even the indios, think that to rape is to be manly? Don't they know that it is the act of a coward? Only a craven who can find no other way to vent his anger-at women resorts to rape."

"That is a thoughtful observation, Capítan," Morales declared.

"Forgive me, I grow philosophical when I should not. I—"

A knock interrupted Sandoval's words.

"Come in," Morales barked.

Greater light showed now and revealed the tired, haggared features of Eli Holten. He paused a moment on the threshold, allowing his eyes to adjust to the brightness. Then he stepped fully into the room.

"Captain Sandoval? I was told I could find him here." Fatigue told clearly in Holten's speech.

Sandoval's eyes narrowed at closer examination of Eli and he spoke harshly. "I am Capítan Sandoval of the Federales. Are you one of the —"

"I am Eli Holten. I'm a civilian contract scout on extended leave from the headquarters of General George Crook, United States Army." Holten rushed his words, determined to get them all out before exhaustion overtook him. "Five other Americans and I recently escorted Señorita Esmeralda Escobar to her father's *estancia* west of here."

"This is . . . somewhat unusual, I would say," Captain Sandoval responded pensively.

Curro Morales brightened. "That's right. I remember you now, only clean-shaven and with a wagon. It was said you fought off Apaches and El Gallo de Chaparal."

"Correct. Now El Gallo has banded together with a force of renegade Americans. They have Rancho Fortunado under siege."

"*¡Por dios!*" Sandoval exploded. "I came here to deal with the grin—ah, Americans. You say they are some three leagues west of here?"

"That's right. There are plenty of men fighting them, but they're low on ammunition."

Eyes bright with anticipation of battle, Sandoval began to plan aloud. "You need some rest, naturally. That will come first. Then I'll arrange for an ammunition supply, assemble my men and we can push on. By forced march we should arrive there within two days of now. Then we can crush the bandits against the walls of the hacienda."

Fidel Ocampo had grown impatient at all the waiting and planning. Quietly he sent his men to the west side of the compound, a few departing at different times. They took along the scaling ladders. Satisfied that he had so far managed his scheme undetected, El Gallo led the last contingent away from camp.

"He's gonna get a lot of them boys killed for nothin'," Dave Denton observed after Ocampo's departure.

"Look at it this way, Dave," T. Luther Hayden said lightly. "That means so many less for us to have to deal with after we take the ranch."

Unaware of his partner's cynical attitude, El Gallo made the long circuit to where the bandit gang waited. Each man already knew what he was expected to do. Unlike Hayden, El Gallo had no concern for the damage fire would cause. Stacks of torches had been made ready to be sloshed with kerosene and ignited. The ladders had been sneaked to within two hundred feet of the wall. The lust for gold burned brightly in his men's eyes.

"We are ready," El Gallo pronounced. "The attack will be carried off tomorrow at sunrise. Then we will show the gringo, Hayden, what sort of stuff we are made of. When *we* open the gates to welcome *him*, he'll lose a lot of that arrogance."

El Ojo produced a smile. "I made a bet with myself as to when you would grow tired of playing errand boy for the gringo loco. I'm happy to say that I won."

Ocampo shot him a sideward glance. He didn't quite know how to take that. "He is, you know. Crazy, I mean. He talks of building empires. I may be what some call me, a bandit, a criminal, but that is because Diaz oppresses the people to enrich the few. I know our country's history. Something that apparently Señor Hayden does not. I was a boy of eight when Don Porferio smashed the French and had Maxmillian executed. We Mexicans do not take kindly to the idea of emperors."

Beltran's eyes registered his astonishment at such eloquence. "I, too, remember that day. There were clouds, a heaviness in the air, a storm building. Much like today. We stood there barefoot in the mud, you and I, while they brought him out. I held your hand while the tension grew and they gave the orders. '*Carga . . . Al punto . . . ¡Fuego!*'" It seemed the fatal shots echoed off the hills behind them.

"We embraced each other," El Gallo took up the narrative. "And gulped fast and hard to keep from throwing up at the sight of all the blood that sprayed from Maxmillian's back. Ah, but we're older now and these are different days."

"De veras, hermano," Beltran agreed. "With new battles to be fought. Everything is in place as you wished."

"Then let's get it going."

Eli Holten rode at the head of the column with Captain Sandoval. They had first heard gunfire some fifteen minutes ago. Sandoval had immediately ordered the column to a fast canter. Over the thunder of hoofbeats they could still hear occasional flat thumps when the cannon of Rancho Fortunado discharged. At Holten's suggestion the troops changed direction, to circle the bandit camp and come immediately to the relief of the beleaguered hacienda. One more low swale and they would be on top of the fighting, Eli registered.

"We're getting close," he shouted to Capt. Sandoval.

The Federale officer nodded. "These lances are pretty things. Nearly of no use at all." Then he offered a wolfish grin. "If we catch them on the ground though, it can be some sport."

At the top of the rise they saw men rushing the wall. Sandoval turned slightly in the saddle. "Couch . . . lances! Right and left echelon. Lower . . . tips! CHARGE!"

Eli Holten had his Winchester ready when the entire line bolted into a gallop. It would do little good, he realized, firing from a plunging horse. Yet a mental victory could be won over the enemy when they realized that the *lanceros* were so supremely confident that only one man wielded a firearm.

Barely had the first bright notes spilled from the bugle when El Gallo's bandits realized they had been hit in the rear. Several turned about, jaws agape, eyes bulging in fear. The rippling line of lances drew nearer. Ladders leaned against the wall in several places and men continued to swarm over into the compound. Even this success began to falter, although the firing dwindled from the defenders as they ran out of ammunition. Swiftly the Federale lancers closed on their foe.

Shrieks of mortal agony filled the air as the steel tips of the slender lances slid into flesh. Here and there a lance pulled free. More often they broke off. Abondoning their damaged weapons, the lanceros drew huge horse pistols from saddle holsters and fired point-blank into the upturned, fear-filled faces of the bandits. Eli Holten reined in and began to selectively shoot men off the ladders. He ran the magazine dry and began to shuck fresh rounds into the tube. A bullet cracked past so close to his ear that it temporarily deafened him. Powder smoke made his eyes water.

"¡Aqui! ¡Reuniemos aqui!" a deep voice bawled. Survivors on the ground began to rally at the indicated place. Holten stuffed another cartridge into his Winchester and took aim at the center of the regrouping men. He loosed a round that ripped skin and bone from the top of El Ojo Beltran's right shoulder. Eli cycled the lever action and took steadier aim. He seemed to see the bandit lieutenant's eyes widen as though in recognition of his end a moment before the flash and smoke obscured Eli's vision.

When he could see again, El Ojo Beltran lay sprawled on the ground, a third of his head blown away by the .44 slug. The regrouping he had begun dissolved in a flurry of shots from the Federales. First one, then a second bandit set out running toward the outlaw camp. Five joined here, then a dozen more.

From inside the compound cries for mercy and offers of surrender came from the nearly victorious bandits. Loathe to let it end there, Eli singled out Captain Sandoval and rode to him.

"Remember the Gatling gun," he said tersely. "We had better attack the bandit camp before the shock effect wears off and they get it into operation."

Sandoval nodded grimly. He'd heard of the rapid-fire, repeating guns, though had never seen one. If they could do what this man Holten said, not even his men could be made to keep ranks facing it.

"Mother of God, what's that?" Clarence Eagen blurted at the sounds of renewed fury from the distant battle.

"I think it safe to say that our Mr. Holten managed to find reinforcements," T. Luther Hayden said dryly. "I have to admire that boy's courage in maintaining to the end that Holten returned to the hacienda. Even I began to believe him. Now it seems we are in considerable trouble. Grab what you can. We must get out of here quickly as possible."

Before food, water and other supplies had been loaded on pack animals, and their riding stock saddled, the first of El Gallo's deserters streamed back into camp. The Federales raced after them. T. Luther Hayden had not even swung astride his dun lineback when the deadly ring of soldiers closed around, sealing off any hope of quick escape.

"The Gatling gun," Hayden suggested around the stub of a cigar in his thin lips.

Three men made a try for the impressive weapon, only to die within five steps. Well-aimed shots cut down two more who ran toward the waiting piece. Well-disciplined, the lancers sat their horses, impassively examining the cornered enemy. At a signal from Capt. Sandoval, additional band instruments appeared. A drum roll began, then a trio of trumpets blazed in the midday sun.

"*Taaa-ta-da Taaa-taa!*" the first notes blared ominously.

El Gallo Ocampo and a dozen of his men removed their hats and solemnly crossed themselves. Their blank faces held only a hint of the terror they felt. Angered by this, more than the appearance of the Federales, T. Luther snarled at them.

"What is this? Are you afraid of a little bit of music?"

"No, Señor Hayden," El Gallo answered him in a small, fearful voice. "Not just any bit of music. *This* music. It is *el Deguello*, the *No-Quarter*."

The alto trumpet started its first, chilling upward trill.

"Some call it the Cut-throat Song."

"It's still just a piece of silly music," Hayden persisted.

"Perhaps, Señor. But Santa Anna had it played for those gringos in the Alamo Mission. It means that even if we try, our surrender will not be accepted. Not a one of us will leave here alive."

CHAPTER 19

Silence, except for the mourning of the women, hung over the hacienda. Eli Holten rode in to subdued cheers. Don Francisco, he discovered, had received a slight wound and rested in his bed. Eli was saddened to learn that Ed Hendrickson had died in this most recent attack. That left only Luke Walker. Eli took him aside.

"Luke, round up all of the *vaqueros* able to ride. We brought plenty of ammunition. I want us to ride out and help finish this thing. Captain Sandoval of the Federales agreed to surround the outlaws and wait for our arrival."

Luke grinned below his flowing mustache. "Sounds good to me. You'd better see Miz Wallis. Say a few words to comfort her. She's mighty broke up over Ed."

"I can well imagine," Eli agreed. He found Joan on a circular bench under an olive tree. Esmeralda sat with her, patting Joan's shoulder and letting her cry out her misery.

"He saved the lives of three children," Esmeralda told Eli. "Some of the bandit *cabrónes* broke through into the inner garden. They found the children and were going to kill them. Ed discovered it and shot one of them. It was his last bullet. After that he went for

201

them, using his rifle as a club. He got another, split his skull with the stock, but . . ." Esmeralda bit her lower lip and tears slid from under closed lids. "But before he could reach the third, the bandit shot him twice in the belly."

Eli, always uncomfortable comforting others, patted Wallis lightly on one shoulder. "We'll see that they pay for it, Joan. Trust me, I'll take care of it personally."

"You've arrived just in time," Captain Sandoval greeted Eli Holten cordially.

The makeshift band still played the Cut-throat Song. Eli took note of it, the haunting melody giving him chills. He nodded toward the outlaws below. "Let's get this thing over."

"Every other man will charge down on them. When they have passed through and returned to our lines, the other number will do the same. We will continue until there is no enemy left."

"Not even one or two to hang?" Eli inquired. The concept of no quarter was alien to him. He found it somewhat lacking in respectability.

Sandoval sensed this. "They have until the music stops to surrender. El Gallo and his men know that for a certainty. The others do by now. We have been playing for half an hour. If they wish to take their chances with the courts, all they need do is lay down their arms and walk up toward us."

Sporadic sniping began before Eli could answer. "In other words, it's their choice whether to make a final, defiant stand or to give up?"

"Correct, Señor Holten."

"In that case, I'd like to be on the first charge

202

against them."

"Oh? I had the feeling you disapproved."

"I still have my reservations," Eli admitted. "Only there's a couple of them down there with whom I want to make a personal satisfaction."

"As you wish," Sandoval informed him.

Sandoval raised his watch and made an ostentatious display of looking at the face. It chimed a scrap of Brahms while the cover was open, a chilling contrast to the blood-thirsty music in the background. The Mexican officer made a chopping motion with one hand and the *Deguello* cut off instantly. The sniping ceased also. A long, tense silence followed.

It stretched on for five minutes, ten, twenty. The men below began to nervously handle their weapons. Sandoval raised in his stirrups and turned slightly so all could hear.

"Odd numbers, draw . . . pistols. Even numbers stand fast."

Once more silence held. Out of range for all but the best of rifles, the two contending units could do nothing else. After five nerve shredding minutes, Sandoval bellowed mightily.

"Prepare . . . to . . . charge." Muffled now, the drums began to roll. "CHAAARRRRGE!"

Winchester ready, Eli Holten brought Sonny to a gallop. The slight slope that led downhill to the outlaw camp made excellent ground to carry a cavalry assault and for a wild moment Eli's heart sang with the exhiliration he had experienced during his first years with the 12th U.S. Cavalry at Fort Rawlins. Not wont to die like cattle in a slaughter house, Eli noticed, the colorfully dressed bandits of Fidel Ocampo sprang to their mounts and made a concentrated rush at a single point. They had experienced Federale tactics before, he felt certain. Eli reined in and dismounted.

Rifle steady, he took careful aim on first one bandit then another. He had to break the strength and impetus of their charge or they would batter a hole in the line wide enough to allow all of the outlaws to escape. Their apparent terror at the sound of *el Deguello* was a sham, he realized suddenly. Sandoval's smugness should have tipped him off that this was a favorite ploy, one that had worked in the past and the innate conservative nature of the military officer corps would not concede had been overcome by domestic troublemakers.

After all, it was a Mexican device of war, designed to strike fear in the hearts of their enemies, not in Mexicans themselves, Eli reasoned. No wonder Ocampo had earned such a fearsome reputation from his previous encounters with the federal police militia. Another bandit dropped and Eli levered in a new cartridge. He made a note to point out this new intelligence to Sandoval after the battle. Then he set to replacing spent ammunition.

"I think . . . he's going to . . . make it work," T. Luther Hayden stated with growing enthusiasm. He watched El Gallo's charge through field glasses. Though dust and smoke rose to mask the scene, Luther had observed enough to realize that El Gallo had known what he talked about.

"They actually believe that music'll scare somebody, huh?" Quint Rhalls sneered.

"It scared the piss right outta me," Willie Harker admitted. "I had to take a leak four times while they was playin' it."

"Mount up, men," T. Luther commanded. "Get

ready to ride at a gallop the minute the Mexicans hit that Federale line."

"¡*Dios!* These bandits can really fight," a young lieutenant in Captain Sandoval's command shouted to a lancer close by.

"It's true I didn't expect this from them," the youthful private responded.

The two lines had clashed, recoiled momentarily, then flung themselves at each other again. At the last moment El Gallo had concentrated his front to a narrow point, only four men wide. Two of those fell in the first encounter, to be replaced by another pair. With closed, tight faces, sweating under the morning sun, they cut their way through the line with sixguns and knives. A dozen poured through while the gap widened to left and right. Then the bandits began to spread out and engage the Federales from the rear. Hayden's American outlaws arrived a moment later.

Caught between two waves of desperate men, the federal militiamen abandoned their attack and sought to save themselves. Relief from their comrades was too many precious seconds away. At a signal from the center of the milling bandits, the fighting broke off and the once easy prey strung out in a mad flight toward the second line of troops and the distant mountains beyond.

From his vantage point, Eli Holten saw the rapid change in initiative. When the apparently blindly fleeing bandits concentrated into a spearhead drive at the last thin line of the Federales, it took only seconds for Eli to identify the source of control. He changed his point of aim to a tight cluster of men in the center of the V-shaped formation.

Two fell from their horses, and a third slumped forward, wounded, before the Winchester ran out of ammunition. The scout spat a harsh word, scabbarded his rifle and swung into the saddle. With an unfamiliar Colt '73 sixgun in his hand, he started toward the enemy column. Not wearing the tan uniform of the Federales gave him a sort of protective coloration. He was in among the bandits before anyone noted his presence. One of the bandits noted his blond hair and Anglo features.

"Who's that?" he demanded.

Right then Hayden's American brigands again joined the advance force and pushed in among them. Lupe Mendez saw this and answered the curious one. "It is only one of the gringos."

Carried along by the impetus of the break-out, Eli Holten rode with the outlaws. Weapons blazed from both sides and now behind. Taking only minor risks, Eli worked his way closer to where Fidel Ocampo directed the bold escape. Even here in the midst of the fleeing band men discharged their firearms. The scout worked within twenty feet of Ocampo when the bandit chief looked to his left.

Fidel Ocampo instantly recognized the big, broadshouldered frame of Eli Holten. He filled his lungs to bellow his discovery when his gaze locked on the rising black muzzle of Eli's Colt. The forty-five caliber revolver developed a tongue of yellow-orange flame and white hot agony erupted in Ocampo's chest. In the wild melee, no one noticed that their leader had been shot, let alone from where the bullet had come.

A horse could not have kicked him so hard, Fidel Ocampo marveled a second before spreading numbness blocked out all pain. Immediately, Eli Holten worked his way in closer to deliver a final shot. Eyes milky and somewhat glazed studied his approach. When Eli brought the sixgun up part way, Fidel raised a restraining hand.

"Do not bother," Fidel Ocampo spoke breathily, a pink foam forming on his lips. "You've killed me fair, gringo. I'm shot through both lungs. I've never . . . never known a man . . . before who . . . who could best me. *Vaya con dios, gringo.*"

"And you, too," Eli Holten found himself saying without having planned it.

Ocampo heaved his thick shoulders and tried to straighten. *"Pater noster qui est in cielis,"* he began to recite in the remembered Latin of his childhood. A mighty sigh, more a convulsion, shook him and he slumped forward, to slide off his line-back dun under the milling hoofs of the band.

Clear now of the Federale line, Eli Holten looked around and did some fast thinking. *"¡El jefe!"* he shouted in Spanish. "The Federales have killed el jefe!"

Instantly organization dissolved among the Mexican bandits. Abandoning their formation they streaked for the protection of the hills, Hayden's Americans streaming out behind.

"Where is the Señor Holten?" Captain Sandoval demanded once he had reorganized his troops for pursuit.

"He, ah, he attacked the center of the bandido force, sir," the first sergeant replied. "I have asked and men tell me that they last saw him headed for El Gallo. It may be he is the one who killed Ocampo. If so, the rest have not recognized him . . . or we would have found his body."

"Ummmm," Sandoval murmured contemplatively.

After several moments, the Federale officer gestured to the battlefield. "Leave a detail to gather all the dead. Collect their weapons and belongings and make a list. The rest of us will ride out after those who escaped."

Eli Holten let himself drift back into the rear ranks of the fleeing Americans. There was less possibility of being detected there, he considered. The miles fled away under the hoofs of their horses. All the while, Eli proposed and rejected plans for turning this escape into defeat. Isolated as he was he had no help upon which he could rely. He also had little chance of killing Hayden and getting away with a whole skin. All he could do, he at last accepted, was string along and wait for a situation to suggest itself. At the point where three streams formed the headwaters of the river, the outlaws halted.

"That little abandoned town can't be more than two miles from here," T. Luther Hayden informed his followers. "We'll hole up there and see if the Federales are coming after us. If they do hit us, we'll have far better protection in those buildings than out in the open. That Gatling ought to give us the edge."

"The Gatling gun took a hell of a pounding coming this far on its own wheels, T. Luther," Grover Hanks advised him. "With that, an' its regular crew dead, I don't know how much use it's gonna be."

"We'll *make* it work for us," T. Luther insisted. "We've got a fair lead, so we can afford to slow down a little. Dave," he addressed to Dave Denton, "when we get to that village, pick some men and start figuring out the Gatling gun."

"You' got it, boss," Dave replied cheerfully.

For a while, Eli Holten considered killing Dave as his first move. Then he rejected the idea. He'd be shot to doll rags before he got to whatever he decided to be second. Hat brim pulled low, he hung back as far as he could without attracting attention. Half an hour's ride over the narrow, rough mountain trail brought them to the empty village.

At once, T. Luther set about establishing a defensive position. Four men were assigned to the church, to establish a lookout post in the bell tower. Three would rest while the fourth watched. After a short while, Eli joined them, saddle bags over one shoulder, Winchester in his left hand.

"Boss said I should come along, too," he informed the outpost occupants.

One gave him a hard, speculative look. "Don't recall seein' you before," he began.

"I'm new. Came in with the other Texas boys and that fast-shootin' gun," Eli invented.

"Ummm. Good enough, then. What say you take first watch, while we check out this place?"

"If that's the way you want it," Eli responded with a shrug.

Rubbing palms together, he started up the board strip ladder to the belfry. Below, the others set about exploring the church. Twenty minutes later, excited shouts came from under the vestry floor. Those looking elsewhere on the church grounds ran to discover the cause.

Grinning broadly, two of the outlaws climbed out of a cellar. Each holding a pair of green, corked bottles. They had another two stuffed into the waistbands of their trousers.

"Lookie what we found. Those padres sure take

209

care of their wine."

"Lemme have some," one hardcase demanded.

"We oughtta tell the others," a third suggested.

"There ain't enough to go around, dummy. Why share our secret?"

Greedy grins went the rounds. "Hey, you in the tower. I'll send you up one," one of the discoverers offered.

Eli peered over the square-cut hole in the floor. "Obliged." He'd rather they sloshed it all down, but to refuse might create undue interest.

In due time, the youngest of the four men below, a boy in his late teens, climbed the ladder and delivered a bottle to Eli. Then he took a look around.

"Gol-dang. You can see forever up here," he remarked. The realization of height suddenly assailed him and he grasped the framed opening for support.

"I ain't never been this high before. Sorta takes yer breath away."

"Look at the inside wall. And at the floor," Eli suggested. "When you set your feet on the top rung, keep on looking straight ahead of you. Whatever you do, don't look down."

The kid froze. "I-I—I don't th-think I can do it," he moaned.

About the last thing Eli needed was the young outlaw up there with him while he was on lookout. Considering the effort to change that, he relented.

"Sit down. Put your back to the outside wall and look at the one opposite you. Keep on doing that until you can close your eyes." Clumsily he helped the boy into position. Eli could feel the lad's rapid heartbeat through the cloth of his shirt.

Half an hour passed and the young gunman appeared a bit less pale around the lips. He could still not look at the hole in the floor. Eli shifted position and pulled field glasses from his saddle bags. Slowly he scanned the rocky hillsides. After a moment he nodded in satisfaction. His eyes had not been tricking him. Short, brown men in tan uniforms flitted between the larger boulders, advancing on the village. Off to his left he saw the scratch crew for the Gatling gun attempting to figure out their new weapon.

Despite the damage it had sustained, the rapid-fire piece functioned properly when the crank was turned. The question remained whether it would be effective against the assault he saw developing. Eli watched while Dave Denton inserted the inward slanting lips of the magazine and snapped the heavy metal box in place. The long, lanky gunhawk stepped behind the Gatling and reached for the crank. He experimentally swung the barrel unit on its pentel and then began to turn the big handle.

Metallic rattling came from the Gatling. Then the first .45-70 round detonated. A second, third, fourth, fifth, sixth, seventh, to a continuous roar, incapable of being counted. Slugs screamed off the boulders outside town. Eli took a quick look in that direction. The Federales had all dropped to the ground. The firing stopped and the last ricochet moaned away through the mountain pass. Laughing and shouting, the neophyte gun crew congratulated themselves. Slowly the Federales came to low crouches and began to advance.

By sheer good fortune, not a one had been struck by a bullet, Eli noted. He felt a tugging at his shirt sleeve. Eyes screwed tightly shut in a pallid face, the boy outlaw clutched at him.

"What was that?"

"The new crew was testing the Gatling gun," Eli

told him.

The kid sighed in relief, though his eyes remained tightly closed. "I—I was afraid we were attacked."

"Nothing like that. You ready to climb down now?" Eli asked.

"N-no. I c-can't do it. I can't even open my eyes," the youth pleaded.

Bad news for him to stay here. Though with his eyes closed, Eli considered, he would not be much of a threat. A quick look showed the Federales to be within thirty yards of the outermost buildings. Eli quickly decided to take out the Gatling crew first. He hefted his rifle and took aim as the first clear notes sounded on a bugle.

"¡Ataque! ¡Asaltanos los edificios!" The cry rippled across the hillside.

"What's going on?" the youthful outlaw demanded in a fearful tone.

"Keep quiet and keep your head down," Eli Holten commanded.

Then the scout set his sights on Dave Denton at the Gatling gun and took the slack from his trigger.

CHAPTER 20

Mountain silence turned to bedlam when the Federales rose up and began firing as they rushed forward on foot. Quickly as the barrels could revolve, six rounds ripped from the Gatling. Then a .44 slug from Eli Holten's Winchester smacked into the point of Dave Denton's shoulder. It slammed him off balance and his jangled nervous system completed the job as he jerked backward and flopped on the ground.

Dave's howl of pain turned to a liquid gurgle as blood flowed into his left lung. By then Eli had chambered another round and put a bullet through the left ear of the assistant gunner. Gagging and wailing in horror, the man dropped the ammunition can and ran blindly into the town. Eli's third sizzling projectile smashed into the side of the magazine, disabling it like the one it had replaced. Even with a new gunner, the terrible weapon would not fire again.

"Wh-who'er you shootin' at?" the disoriented young gunhawk asked.

"Federales," Eli lied. "All of a sudden they popped up out of the rocks."

The kid's face crumpled and for a moment, Eli thought he would cry. "It's all my fault. Because I got

213

scared of the height. I—I gotta help you," he concluded, coming to his knees.

"Sorry, kid," Eli told him a moment before he solidly planted the curved brass butt plate of his Winchester against the hinge point of the boy's jaw. Funny thing, the scout thought a moment later, he meant it.

Federale bullets began to smack into the plastered adobe front of the church. It had become too hot for Eli to lend any aid. Several of the less sturdily built buildings had burst out in flame. Thatch roofs caught from sparks. Here and there men fell back, firing at only partly seen targets among the buff rocks. A clammer from below drew Eli's attention.

"Give some coverin' fire up there. A bunch of the boys is headed this way."

"You've got it," Eli responded.

He quickly sighted on the most distant forms of the outlaws and opened up on them. Firing as they ran, Federales closed in on the town from three sides. A sheer drop of a thousand feet waited on the fourth. A flaming shed crashed in on itself and sent a shower of sparks skyward.

"This way, boys," Eli heard the familiar voice of T. Luther Hayden from the street below. "Into the church. We'll make our stand here. The walls are thick enough we can hold out forever."

"Bring water," another outlaw voice urged. "Lots of it. And all the food you've got."

Eli saw an outlaw laboring unsteadily along the steep street with two goatskins of water over his shoulders. The scout neatly shot the skins first, then put a bullet in the man's chest. In the midst of the tumult, the kid came feebly back to consciousness. Fighting back his earlier fear, he rose to his knees and

214

managed to look out in time to see the direction the scout had been firing. Numb with shock and pain from the butt stroke, he bent double and shouted weakly down the central opening.

"Hey, this guy up here's shootin' at our bunch."

Fumbling, he clumsily tried to draw his sixgun. Startled exclamations and shouted orders came from below. The kid cleared leather a moment before Eli Holten slammed the butt of his Winchester into the shallow chest. Propelled backward, the boy loosed a round that struck the inside of the bell's curved surface before he plummeted, screaming, down the tower. He hit the tile floor with a bone-crushing splat.

"My God," one of the hardcases gulped.

"Who is it up there?" another demanded.

A third grabbed the bell rope and began to vigorously yank on it. Slowly the crown began to rotate away from the tilting direction of the leader and lip. The clapper swayed and leaned toward the closer edge. Quickly the man released the rope and the crown stock swung rapidly the opposite direction. With calamitous clangor, the clapper struck and the mighty bell sounded.

Counter-motion had already set in and the enterprising outlaw hauled on the rope again to aid it. Once more the bell sounded, inches from the scout's ears. Vibrations of the resonating bronze set the scene around him wavering and he staggered hazardously close to one of the four openings. Again! Sheer volume of sound threatened to rip Eli Holten's sanity from his head. He fought to find reason and direction.

Fumbling, his hand encountered the coffin handle of his Bowie knife. Mind lagging behind conditioned muscles, he drew it and began to hack at the rope binding on one side of the stock. Desperately slow the strands began to part. The bell thundered in his head again.

More fibres parted under the keen edge. Yarns began to unravel. Strands pinged apart silently in the awesome presence of the bell's tone. At last the rope parted and the accursed noisemaker hung askew in its cradle. Ignoring snapping bullets from below and outside, Eli hurried to the opposite side and began cutting. With the aid of the bell he soon had three strands parted. Determined to drive the enemy from the tower the hardcase below below yanked on the rope once more.

With a loud pop, the bindings parted and the bell plunged downward, clanging mournfully in its death crash. Bits of wood, where the stock or lip struck, preceded it. Men cried out in alarm.

Too late for two of them, who shrieked in terrible agony when the ponderous casting dropped on them, severing their bodies in twain at the waist.

"I'll get that son of a bitch," T. Luther Hayden snarled, climbing over the tatters of corpses, shattered tile, and broken wood.

With determined energy he began to climb the ladder. Above, Eli Holten blasted three shots from his Winchester downward. They missed and he withdrew when answering fire buzzed close by his head. Holten delved into his pocket and produced a stub of cigar. This he ignited. Then he hefted one of the spherical grenades he had earlier taken from his saddle bags.

He touched the fuse with the glowing cigar tip. Biting his lower lip, he counted down until half the fuse had burned. Then he dropped it over the edge of the access hole.

T. Luther Hayden wailed in helpless horror as the hand bomb plummeted past his face. "Oh, my Go—!" It went off at waist level.

Blood and guts showered the men below. Few reacted to the offal, as bits of shrapnel shredded their bodies also. Acrid smoke and fumes rose in the bell tower. Eli Holten staggered back and waved his arms from the open arch.

"Captain Sandoval!" He called. A moment later he repeated. "I think you can come in and clean up now."

Firing dwindled. "What about the American outlaw, Hayden?"

Eli gave that some thought. "He's . . . not . . . all together any more," he replied, head still throbbing from the clanging bell and punishing blast.

They returned to Rancho Fortunado. The Federales rode in tightly disciplined ranks. The *vaqueros* and tradesmen of the ranch galloped about wildly, whooped and shouted about their victory. Eli Holten accompanied Captain Sandoval. The old *haciendado* received them in a small drawing room off his bed chamber.

"Don Francisco, the outlaws have been destroyed," Captain Sandoval reported. "Both the *Norteños* and the unsavory band of Fidel Ocampo. Your friend here, Señor Holten, personally disposed of both leaders. It's been an entirely satisfactory campaign."

"Thank you, Captain. I can happily report that I am on the mend. Enough so that I insist you and your men remain here to rest from your exertions and to let us honor you with a special fiesta."

217

"You're too kind, Don Francisco. However, we must return to Hermosillo."

"No-no, I insist, Captain Sandoval," Don Francisco countered with a touch of his former resolve.

"When Don Francisco holds a fiesta," Eli Holten advised, "It's a good idea to attend. If you don't, you'll regret it. The food, the drinking, the lovely ladies . . ." he detailed dreamily. He stopped abruptly. "Speaking of lovely ladies, where is Esmeralda?"

Don Francisco smiled broadly. "She said to inform you she will be in the garden."

Eli made his excuses and departed quickly. He soon found her, though not strictly speaking in the garden. She waited Eli's coming on a mossy mound beside the small pond at the corner of the outer walls. Her face flushed with joy as he made his way through the trees. Eli reached her side and knelt there.

"Oh, Eli, I was so worried," she gasped before they embraced.

"I'm safe enough," he assured her. "Except for a few scrapes and an awful ringing in my ears. There was this bell—"

"A bell?" Esmeralda interrupted, eager to hear all. "What has a bell to do with it?"

"I'll tell you about it, later." Then he kissed her. Gently at first, almost brotherly.

Esmeralda's mobile lips and ardent tongue soon changed that. Her hands explored his body, confirming his statement of being sound. She soon found that one part was solid enough, swiftly rising under the teasing touch of her fingers. Eli shifted his position. His hand cupped one firm, up-tilted breast. Esmeralda sighed and fumbled at his fly.

"Remember last time," Eli cautioned, his lips still

218

on hers.

"No worry. I fed Matilda half a bottle of tequila so we could have this moment together."

Eli chuckled throatily. "You think we can get it over in a moment?"

"No. Not if I have my way," Esmeralda responded.

Her feathery touch sent shivers of excitement through Eli's body. He closed his eyes to a symphony of colors. Esmeralda broke their light embrace and a rustle of clothing told of her preparations. When Eli looked again her creamy tan body caught highlights from the twinkling water. She struck a seductive pose, her best charms boldly exhibited for his appreciation.

"You're so lovely it makes me ache," Eli said roughly.

He soon freed himself of buckskin and whipcord and lay beside her, passion ignited as she welcomed him into intimate closeness.

"Of course you're staying for the fiesta, Don Eli," a much improved Don Francisco Escobar declared some two hours later.

"I'm sorry, Don Francisco, but I cannot. We were leaving before, if you recall. I must get back to General Crook's headquarters. Also, it remains for us to get away from the rancho without running into the Apaches who attacked us before. They may have decided that their agreement with me is ended, now that the bandits are subdued."

"I am devastated," the old man declared with a dramatic rolling of his eyes. "What can I say or do to make you change your mind."

"I'm afraid there's nothing, sir," Eli maintained.

219

"I fear I must be terribly frank with you. My sons all have *estancias* of their own, town houses in Hermasillo or Mexico City. One raises fighting bulls near Aguas Calientes. Each is wealthy in his own right. There is no one else in the family to whom I can leave Rancho Fortunado. If my daughter made a suitable marriage, naturally my son-in-law would be a worthy recipient of my property. I am an old man, and perhaps a foolish one, but I'm not blind, Señor.

"I know as well as you that a desirable marriage might not be possible after . . . after the terrible events of Esmeralda's life. Yet, there is one man who filled the expectations of a jealous father exceptionally well. A brave man, a dedicated man, a man I would be proud to call son. I also know that my daughter is most fond of him and he of her."

"Well then, it sounds like your problems can be easily solved," Eli said lightly.

"Not so. This paragon of manhood wants to ride away and play soldier. He prefers to take his chances wth wandering Apaches instead of remaining in a position of substance and influence. That man is *you*, Don Eli."

Eli gasped. Though he tried, words would not come. At last he blurted out, "I, ah, I've . . . never before been proposed to by the father of the prospective bride."

"Perhaps I do things badly," Don Francisco conceded. "I only sought to make you fully aware of the place you have won in my daughter's heart and in mine. All the people of Rancho Fortunado idolize you and would follow your orders without question. Consider it . . . my son."

With great difficulty Eli disengaged himself from the perilous conversation. Being marriage shy, Eli

220

knew he had to escape this only too tempting future, yet he didn't wish to hurt the kindly old *haciendado*. By late afternoon he believed he had struck on the proper way.

After a passionate parting in Esmeralda's bed, Eli left a note explaining that it was his sacred trust to see that the fortunes bestowed by Don Francisco be delivered to the families of those who died in the fighting. He promised to keep in contact and to return when possible. Then he joined his remaining companions, Luke Walker and Joan Wallis.

Together they managed to slip out of the compound shortly after midnight, without being detected. Fifteen minutes after sunrise, Eli Holten measured the distance they covered with considerable satisfaction. They would, he decided, be well into the mountains within three hours. He started to lead out when a gasp and cry from Joan Wallis halted him.

"My God! It's the Apaches again," Joan wailed.

True enough, Eli soon found. The squat, stout warriors lined the ridge in front of them. Others came into view at both sides. Eli quickly sized up their chances. Although willing to die fighting, Eli had a responsibility to the living and the dead. He slid the Winchester from its saddle scabbard.

"Luke, Joan, get ready. We'll take as many as we can, then ride back toward the ranch. It's the only chance we have," he instructed his friends.

"They'll . . . they'll kill us, won't they?" Joan asked in gulps.

"Not if our horses are fresher than theirs. The *vaqueros* will hear the shooting and come to our aid. The Apaches won't get too close to the ranch, you can be sure of that."

With a wild cry and a wave of the arm, the Apache leader signaled a charge. Springing to their horses, the bronze warriors raced frantically down the ridge and across the desert flat. It took only moments for Eli Holten to realize something was out of kilter.

Apaches rarely charged their enemy. Even so, Eli determined to make a good accounting. He raised his Winchester to his shoulder. Before the first shot could be fired, the yipping braves reined in and their leader—Eli recognized Alchise rather than Dos-Tan-Nanta—called to them from a hundred yards distance.

"There was disagreement among us. Dos-Tan-Nanta took two hands of men and left us here. We have been watching your long fight with the bandidos. We're most impressed. We mean you no harm. Can we come closer?"

Eli lowered his Winchester. "You may. Pick three men to accompany you."

At fifty feet, Alchise stopped and spoke again. "Will you take us to the soldier-chief, Crook?"

"Why is that?" Eli asked, genuinely puzzled.

"Will you speak honey words to Crook to get us places as scouts? Will you ask for us that we may be allowed to work under *Ojo de Halcon?*"

"Who?" Eli asked, his confusion growing.

"Why, you, of course. Hawkeye Holten."

Well, Eli figured. He couldn't beat that offer. He'd started out with five white volunteers, lost three, and could now come back with twenty new scouts. Which also took away half of his reason for a hasty departure. An anticipatory smile bloomed on Eli's lips.

"I'll gladly do that, Alchise. Take your men and go north through the mountains. In seven days time I'll meet you at the Big Bend of the Gila River. Ski-Be-

Nan-Ted is waiting there for me now. Tell him what you told me and that I'm coming along behind. Right now my friends and I have a big fiesta to attend.

And a couple more nights with Esmeralda, Eli didn't bother to add.